Praise for the W

No Atta

"Super sweet and swoon-worthy!"

—Jennifer L. Armentrout, #1 *New York Times* bestselling author

"Readers will spend the first half of this story on the edge of their seats and the last half hugging a box of tissues."

—Priscilla Glenn, bestselling author of *Back to You* and *Emancipating Andie*

"Sweet, beautiful, funny, and heartbreaking all rolled into one amazing story."　　　　—Tara Sivec, *USA Today* bestselling author

"Allow me to summarize *No Attachments*: Great story. Amazing characters. Awesome read."　　　—*Book Freak Book Reviews*

"The story itself is heartwarming, which really is a characteristic of a Tiffany King book. Her stories always turn struggles into strength and her characters always find the good. That's one of the reasons I love to read her books. They're real. They're emotional. They're heartwarming."　　　　　　—*Stuck in Books*

"*No Attachments* will leave you more than a little attached to Ashton and Nathan."　　　　—*Book Angel Booktopia*

"Absolutely heartbreakingly beautiful."　　—*Once Upon a Twilight*

continued . . .

"Anyone who loves a great contemporary should check out this title. You'll laugh, you'll swoon, and you'll love these two characters just like I have." —*A Life Bound by Books*

Misunderstandings

"A beautifully woven story of a love that can withstand anything."
—Molly McAdams, *New York Times* bestselling author

"Funny, real, moving, and passionate, *Misunderstandings* is a MUST-READ for New Adult contemporary romance fans."
—Samantha Young, *New York Times* bestselling author

"Sweet and sexy! Great characters and an intriguing romance . . . So good!" —Cora Carmack, *New York Times* bestselling author

No Attachments

A Woodfalls Girls Novel

TIFFANY KING

BERKLEY BOOKS, NEW YORK

THE BERKLEY PUBLISHING GROUP
Published by the Penguin Group
Penguin Group (USA) LLC
375 Hudson Street, New York, New York 10014

USA • Canada • UK • Ireland • Australia • New Zealand • India • South Africa • China

penguin.com

A Penguin Random House Company

Library of Congress Cataloging-in-Publication Data

King, Tiffany.
No attachments / Tiffany King. —First edition.
p. cm. —(A Woodfalls Girls novel)
ISBN 978-0-425-27478-1 (paperback)
1. Runaway women—Fiction.   2. Private investigators—Fiction.   3. Attachment behavior—Fiction.
4. Fathers and daughters—Fiction.   5. Man-woman relationships—Fiction.   6. Love stories.
I. Title.
PS3611.I5863N6 2014
813'.6—dc23
2014002097

PUBLISHING HISTORY
Originally published as an eBook in 2013
Berkley trade paperback edition / August 2014

PRINTED IN THE UNITED STATES OF AMERICA

10   9   8   7   6   5   4   3   2   1

Cover art by Hannes Photo / Imagebrief.
Cover design by Lesley Worrell.
Interior text design by Tiffany Estreicher.

ACKNOWLEDGMENTS

Every story is a journey. A journey shared with those who encourage you, laugh with you, celebrate with you in triumph, and pick you up in failure. I am fortunate to have family and friends who continue to amaze me with their support and love.

No Attachments was a leap of faith, made possible by these people. Thank you to everyone who encouraged me to write this book and to everyone who took a chance and picked it up. Thank you to my husband, who held my hand through the entire process. Thank you to my children, who never complain about my busy schedule. Thank you to my writer friends, who taught me it's normal to feel crazy sometimes.

ACKNOWLEDGMENTS

And finally, a special thank-you to my superhero agent, Kevan Lyon; my editor extraordinaire, Kate Seaver; and my amazing team at Berkley for believing in me. Dreams do come true . . . so dream big.

1. *Why Lightweights Shouldn't Drink*

ASHTON

"Come on, go," my friend Tressa said, trying to push me out of my chair. "What good is a bucket list if you're too chicken to do any of it?"

"Zip it," I said out of the corner of my mouth as I apprehensively eyed the situation in front of me. It seemed like a good idea on paper, but actually committing to it suddenly made me nauseated. I took a long pull of my beer, hoping that would help calm my nerves. "God, that's disgusting." I grimaced as the foul liquid poured down my throat. "I don't know how people drink this crap," I complained, slamming the bottle back down on the table a little harder than I should have.

"You're stalling, Ash. Besides, this was your idea. Pick up a random stranger and bang his socks off," Tressa quipped. "You need to seize the opportunity before someone else does, otherwise you'll be SOL, and your only choice will be Old Man Jones over there," she added, making our friend Brittni snort loudly.

"Shush," I said, elbowing her in the gut. Tressa had one volume level—loud. Her words traveled from our table to the many other patrons throughout the only bar in the sleepy little town of Woodfalls, Maine. Joe's was the hotspot, and Friday was your only good chance to meet someone if you were single and on the prowl, because Saturday was family karaoke night.

"Ow, bitch," Tressa said, rubbing her stomach. "It's not like the grumpy old fart can hear us anyway," she said loudly in his direction.

"Gahhhh, shush, Tressa. He's going to hear you," I said, sliding back down in my seat.

"Chillax, drama queen. He doesn't even have his hearing aid in. Watch," she said, shooting me a mischievous grin. "Hey, Mr. Jones, I really want to blow you," she said loudly.

She managed to get the attention of about a dozen guys with that one, including Mr. Jones, who whirled around, studying us with his beady black eyes. His gray bushy eyebrows came together in a unibrow that looked like a giant caterpillar on his forehead.

Brittni snorted again as she shook with laughter. I squirmed uncomfortably on the hard wooden bench, fighting the urge to point at Tressa like we were in kindergarten and had gotten busted for throwing spitballs or something.

Tressa returned his stare head-on, smiling sardonically until he turned back around.

"Sheesh, girl, you're lucky he didn't take you up on your offer," I said, stifling my own laughter.

"Hey, you never know what he's sportin' in those dusty old overalls." Tressa winked.

"Gross," I shrieked.

Tressa just shrugged, unconcerned. I couldn't help admiring her self-assuredness. She didn't care what people thought about her. She was loud and seriously inappropriate, but hilarious as hell, despite the tight leash her boyfriend tried to keep her on. We'd been friends for only four months, but I had grown quite fond of her in that short period of time. Both she and Brittni had welcomed me into their friendship circle without a second thought. They acted like I belonged. Not because they felt sorry for me or pitied me like everyone else had done for so many years, but because they genuinely seemed to like me. Brittni wasn't as flamboyant or inappropriate as Tressa, but she had a wickedly dry sense of humor that kept people on their toes. And then there was me. I wasn't completely sure what I brought to the group, but that was why I was here. Somewhere over the last five years, I'd forgotten who I really was.

"All right, time to stop stalling. Get off your ass and pick up that tall, dark, he-can-have-my-panties-any-day seximist," Tressa said pointedly, looking at the stranger we'd been eyeing for the last fifteen minutes.

"Maybe I should do something else on my list," I said, pulling a rumpled slip of paper out of my bag while desperately trying to ignore the butterflies that had suddenly decided to hang out in my stomach. I gently smoothed out the creases as I contemplated the items scrawled on the paper.

"You're kidding, right? This town has a population of, like, negative ten, and he's the hottest thing to walk in here in forever. When are you going to have the opportunity to have one night of hot, wild sex with a stranger like that again?"

"That's my point. Don't you find it a little weird that we don't know this guy? This town is pretty much off the beaten path. He could be some mass murderer. How do you know he wouldn't put my head in his freezer or something?"

"Sweetheart, after a night with him, you'll want a freezer to cool you off," Tressa said, eyeing him with open admiration. "Besides, if you don't make your move, I'm totally claiming him," she added, adjusting her shirt so the tops of her ample breasts peeked out from the thin camisole she was wearing under her button-up see-through shirt.

"So, you wouldn't mind that you don't know him and that he could very well chop up your body into a million pieces? Not to mention what Jackson would say if he found out," I said, reminding her of her boyfriend.

"Wow, seriously, chill, Ash. She's just trying to give you a spark. Besides, you were a stranger here once too, and you didn't show your true crazy for a couple days," Brittni teased. "Now get up there and sex that possible serial killer up."

"You two are a riot," I said, choking down the last of my beer, which tasted like elephant piss, or at least what I would assume elephant pee would taste like. "All right, wish me luck," I added, finally sliding out of the booth. "If he chops me up into little pieces, neither of you gets those boots of mine you want so bad," I threatened. I made my way up to the counter, where the object of our interest was perched. Considering my shaky legs, I wasn't exactly as subtle as a prowling jungle cat. Tressa was right. The chance of finding a perfect candidate for a one-night stand was slim to none in a town the size of Woodfalls. Strangers were few and far between. Couple that with the fact that he was drop-dead gorgeous, and his sudden appearance was like a gift from God. Not that good-looking was a pre-requisite. The only requirement I had set was that he know nothing about me or my past. I wanted one night where someone wanted me for me, not because they felt sorry for me.

"Hey, Joe, can I get a shot?" I asked, sliding onto the bar stool next to the tall, dark, panty-dropping-worthy hunk.

"Sure thing, Ashton. How'd you like your beer?" Joe asked, drying a small shot glass with a cotton towel he had tucked into his apron.

"It tasted like pee," I confessed.

Joe threw his head back as a loud roar of laughter erupted out of him. "Drink a lot of pee, do you?" he asked.

I opened my mouth to answer him sarcastically when the object of my fascination let out a low rumble of laughter. Seizing my opportunity, I gulped down the bourbon Joe had placed in front of me and swiveled around to face the stranger next to me. The liquor burned its way down my throat, leaving a fiery trail all the way to my belly, but it was eclipsed by the liquid fire that burned through me when my eyes finally met his.

"Can I get you another?" he asked softly in a radio-DJ-like

voice that you would hear on a lonely Saturday night, encouraging listeners to call in with their favorite weepy love songs.

"Sure." I eyed my empty glass as my body responded to his sexier-than-sin voice. I was a sucker for a deep voice—or an accent, especially British or Australian accents. Neither, though, could compare to the richness of his voice, which seemed to vibrate through me. I realized in that instant that I had left a crucial item off my bucket list. Having an intimate conversation with someone with a voice like his should have topped my list.

"You all right?" he asked, looking bemused as Joe placed another shot in front of me. I started to answer his question and mentally kicked myself when I realized I'd been staring at him like he was a tall glass of water on a hot summer day. Matter of fact, I was about 99.9 percent sure I might have licked my lips in anticipation.

"Absolutely. How 'bout you?" I asked, trying for a seductive throaty voice that just went wrong. "Thanks for the drink," I added, sucking down the liquid confidence in an attempt to calm my frazzled nerves.

His bemused expression turned to outright amusement as he took in my watery eyes, which had resulted from my quick gulping of the whiskey shot. "Another?" he asked with raised eyebrows.

"Why not," I answered, though the room was already tilting slightly. I could count on one hand the number of times I'd actually had a drink before tonight. They all centered on the time my life had slipped drastically off course. I'd gone hog wild for a couple of weeks until I realized drowning my sorrows in alcohol only made me sick and didn't solve anything anyway. After that it wasn't a viable option. Needless to say, my time in high school and college had been pretty lackluster.

Tall, Dark, and Dreamy chuckled softly beside me as he flagged down Joe for another round. Holding up his own shot glass, he waited until I raised mine to meet his, and then winked at me as we clinked glasses. "Damn." My breath hitched. I was a sucker for winking too. Something about it made my stomach tighten up in anticipation and my breath quicken. Not to mention, having Mr. Seximist behind the wink made other areas tighten up too, while a certain other area began to throb. It took me a moment to distinguish the throbbing as desire. My one and only sexual encounter had been four years ago, after prom, and it didn't last long enough to ever cross over into the desire category. It was the means to an end. I had wanted to feel normal just for one night, and by the end of the dance, I finally coaxed Shawn Johnson into ending my virgin status once and for all. He'd resisted the idea at first, but my constant touches and whispered comments finally muddled his brain enough that he caved. The actual act lasted less than two minutes and hurt like a bitch, but in the end, I was glad I'd gone through with it.

It was ironic that one wink by Mr. Voice had me crossing my legs in an attempt to distill the ache that was slowly beginning to radiate between my legs. He'd managed to excite me more in three minutes of flirting than Shawn had done in an entire evening of slow dancing, grinding, and sloppy kisses.

I was pulled away from my thoughts by a low chuckle. *Son of a bitch, not again*, I thought, blanching inwardly. He'd busted me gawking at him like a lovesick teenager again. *Okay, pull it together*, I reminded myself. *Focus on why you're here.* I welcomed the warm buzz from my shot of bourbon and the uncharacteristic confidence that came with it. Licking the last drop of amber liquid off my bottom lip, I watched with satisfaction as his eyes settled on my lips. I could do this.

"You know, you keep winking at girls like that and one of them is bound to take it as an invitation," I said.

"Sweetheart, I only wink at the girls I'm interested in," he answered smoothly, tipping his own glass to his lips.

The desire I had been trying in vain to control unfurled inside me, making my nipples harden beneath the black lace bra I'd had the uncanny foresight to don that evening. The dull ache between my legs morphed into a steady throbbing that even my crossed legs could not ease.

"Is that so?" I asked, arching my eyebrow in what I hoped was a seductive manner.

"It's a fact, sweetheart," he whispered close to my ear.

I clamped my lips together so I wouldn't embarrass myself by moaning out loud as his warm breath rustled the hair at the nape of my neck. I resisted the urge to sweep my long dark hair out of the way to give him more access.

"You're pretty cocky," I said as he signaled Joe for another round. My head was already spinning, but I figured another one couldn't hurt.

"Not cocky, sweetheart, confident," he answered huskily,

reaching for our drinks with one hand when Joe brought them over.

I reached over to relieve him of my glass, but before I could retract my hand with my drink in it, he snagged my pinkie with his. Looking at our now-linked hands, I watched as he slowly raised my hand to his mouth. I gripped the glass tightly as he brushed his lips across my knuckles before releasing my hand.

Suddenly, the drink felt ten times heavier with the sudden absence of his hand. The small shot glass slipped from my fingers, spilling the contents over the bar in front of us.

"You okay?" he asked as I swayed on my bar stool, taking in his slightly blurred features

"Absolutely. I do this all the time," I lied.

"I'm sure," he mocked.

"You can bank—" My retort was cut short when my cell phone chirped in my purse.

"I need to use the ladies' room," I breathed, rising unsteadily to my feet as the floor tilted slightly beneath me. "I'll be right back."

"Do you need some help?" he asked, cocking his eyebrow at me.

"Um, I'm pretty sure I know how to pee on my own," I answered, feeling flustered.

He chuckled. "I meant getting to the bathroom. You looked like you were a bit unsteady there."

"I'm good," I clarified before strutting away. It took all my willpower to keep my gait steady as I made my way across the scuffed wooden floors to the bathroom. Tressa and Brittni were leaning against the bathroom counter waiting for me when I entered. It was all part of the plan we had set up. They were here for the status update.

"So, is he a serial killer?" Brittni asked as I headed for one of the stalls.

"Hold on, I really do have to pee."

"He looks like he's into you," she added, switching on the faucet so I could pee in peace.

"Of course he's into her. She's smoking hot," Tressa interrupted. "I bet he's already suffering from a case of blue balls," she added, laughing as I heard the smacking of flesh.

"Do you always have to be so crude?" Brittni asked, disgusted, as I flushed the toilet and opened the stall door.

"He's not the only one," I muttered, filling the palms of my hands with soap before sticking them under the faucet, which was still running.

"Ooh, things a little damp downstairs?"

"Oh my God, Tressa, seriously?" Brittni said, taking another swipe at her.

"That's one way to say it. Put it this way, he'd slide in pretty damn easy right now, if you know what I mean," I giggled, bracing my hands on the counter as the floor beneath me continued to sway.

"You okay, slick?" Brittni asked, really looking at me for the first time since I'd entered the bathroom.

"Fine," I answered, moving my eyes from the slow-rolling floor.

"She's buzzing," Tressa crowed, taking in my glassy eyes and flushed cheeks.

"I sure am." I cracked up, not entirely sure why I found it so funny.

"Are you sure you're up for this, you lightweight?" Brittni asked, placing her hands on my shoulders so she could study me critically.

"I'm fine, Mom," I teased. "I just decided to take the liquid courage route."

"So, you're going through with it?" she asked, looking worried.

"Duh, that was the plan," Tressa chastised.

"I know, but I thought she'd chicken out," Brittni retorted, like I wasn't even there.

"Hey, standing right in front of you," I said, waving my hands exuberantly in front of them like I was trying to land a plane or something to that effect. "Besides, I have to do it, it's on my list," I pointed out.

"Right, it's on your list. I still think it's ridiculous for someone our age to have a bucket list."

"I told you a million times. It's for a study I'm doing for the master's program I'm hoping to get into," I lied, smiling brightly at her. "It's a study on living life to its fullest in a limited time frame."

"So you've said a hundred times. I just think a study on males that have the best pecs or dreamiest eyes would have been more productive."

"That's so cliché and overdone. Having a nice six-pack

usually translates to 'conceited asshole,'" I answered, sweeping the lip gloss Tressa handed me across my lips. "Thanks," I told her, handing the wand back. I tried not to focus on the irony of my new friends having no qualms about sharing their makeup with me. Back home, most people refused to touch anything I had touched. They were all assholes. What I had wasn't contagious.

"You better get back out there before Mr. Blue Balls thinks you ditched him," Tressa interrupted, giving my back a light shove toward the bathroom door. "Text us if he turns out to be an asshole."

"And make sure he bags his junk," Brittni piped in.

Giggling at their advice, I twisted around before exiting the bathroom and threw my arms impulsively around both their necks. "I love you guys," I said, knocking their heads together from my exuberance.

"Okay, we love you too," Brittni complained, trying to extract my arms.

"Yep, she's toasted," Tressa commented, rubbing her head where it had knocked against Brittni's.

"Maybe we should hang around to make sure she doesn't embarrass herself," Brittni mused.

"No way, you guys promised," I reminded them. "If I'm doing this, I'm going in without a safety net."

"Fine, but your scrawny ass better text us first thing tomorrow morning, or we're sending out the armed forces to take down Mr. Seximist," Brittni warned, giving me a quick hard hug.

"Don't worry, Brit, he looks harmless enough. Besides, I've taken at least twenty pictures on my phone. We'll nail that bastard's ass to the wall if he hurts her," Tressa said from behind me as I pushed open the bathroom door.

"Don't worry, my head will make a beautiful mantelpiece," I threw over my shoulder as I sashayed across the room toward the bar.

"Hey, stranger," I said, boldly sliding onto my bar stool.

"Whoa there," Mr. Hotness said as my ass misjudged the middle of the seat and teetered on the edge, making the legs of the stool wobble. Hotness reached over and grasped my arm to steady me.

"You're hot."

"Why thank you," he said, chuckling.

"I mean, your hands are hot . . . no, I mean, your touch is hot . . . shit. Never mind," I mumbled as he chuckled next to me.

"It's not the first time I've been called hot, sweetheart."

"Vanity isn't a virtue," I pointed out, picking up the shot glass that had magically filled itself in my absence. "So, what do you do, Mr. I Know I'm Hot?" I asked, realizing that in all our flirting we'd neglected to exchange names.

"Nathan," he answered, holding out his hand for me to shake.

"Ashton," I parroted as his hand engulfed mine. His touch was sure and sensual at the same time, making my poor hand feel bereft once he let go.

"I'm a freelance journalist."

"Freelance journalist? What does that entail?" I asked, intrigued.

"Lots of traveling and a knack for being able to dig out the truth. I've been fortunate enough to be able to pick my assignments," he answered, turning on his bar stool to face me. His knees knocked against mine, which my body was keenly aware of as our legs settled, intimately touching each other. "I'm actually on my way to my next assignment. What about you?"

"Right now, I'm working at Smith's General Store over on the corner of Main and Stetson," I answered defensively, waiting for his judgments. I didn't bother to mention the barely dried ink on my BA in human psychology, or the fact that up until four months ago, I had been planning my internship at the local hospital back home. Those were need-to-know facts that he didn't need to know.

"I think I met the owner when I arrived today. Fran, right? She's quite an old card," he replied warmly, surprising me.

"Yeah, she is. Don't let her age fool you. She's sharper than people a quarter of her age. That store has been in her family for more than a hundred years. Each generation it's passed down to the next. Fran should have passed it down, like, fifteen years ago, but she claims hell will freeze over before she allows her 'sniveling, no-good, lazy nephew to run it into the ground.' She says she reckons she'll stay until she breathes her last breath or her nephew finally decides to man up. She says she won't be holding her breath on the latter . . ." I rambled on. Obviously, the multiple shots had turned my tongue into a nonstop chattering mess.

"That sounds like the person I met," he said, chuckling softly. "So, have you lived here all your life?" he asked.

Running my finger around the small base of the shot glass, I weighed his question, contemplating how I wanted to answer. "No. I moved here four months ago after my dad died," I lied, giving him the standard answer I'd given everyone else when I moved to town.

"Really?" he asked, studying me critically.

I was slightly taken aback by his response. I'd been greeted with nothing but sympathy when I'd let the lie slip on previous occasions. I always felt a twinge of guilt over it but knew in the end it was necessary. "It was quite sudden," I answered defensively.

"I'm sorry for your loss," he replied, finally offering up the words that I had grown accustomed to hearing.

"Thanks," I said, not sure if his sympathy was genuine. Maybe he really was some psycho who traveled through small towns collecting heads and storing them in his trunk. I sucked down the contents of my glass once again. My brain was teetering on the edge of remaining focused on the noticeably rock-hard pecs beneath his shirt and becoming drowned by the liquor party that was flowing through my bloodstream. My tongue became numb while the buzzing in my head intensified, making me wish I could rest it on the bar. I contemplated climbing up on the bar so I could lie down, but even that seemed like way too much work. Instead, I tried to focus on my last coherent thought, knowing it had something to do with my head.

"Are you going to put your trunk in my head?" I asked, finally able to make my tongue work.

"Excuse me?" he asked, amused.

"Wait. I mean, are you going to put your trunk in me?" I asked, though the question still seemed slightly off.

"Is that what the kids are calling it now?" he asked with open amusement.

"Wait. What did I say?" I asked, shaking my head in a feeble attempt to clear it.

"Well, darling, you asked if I was going to stick my trunk in you. Is that an invitation?"

"Well, shit. I meant, are you going to put my head in your trunk?" I asked slowly, making sure the word placement was correct.

"Just your head?"

"Unless you keep the whole body, but won't your trunk get full if you keep the whole body?" I reasoned, pleased that I was able to form a coherent question even if it was related to my decapitation.

"I'm more a breast kind of guy," he said, smirking.

Laughter bubbled up out of me. "So, your trunk is full of boobies?" I asked, giggling uncontrollably.

"Boobies?" he snorted. "I haven't heard that word in, like, twenty years."

"Twenty years? How old are you?" I asked, giggling again at the idea that my one-night stand would be with an old man.

"Twenty-nine. What about you?"

"Twenty-nine? That's not old."

"Who said I was old?"

"Didn't you?" I asked, confused over why I had thought he was old.

"I only said I haven't heard them called 'boobies' in twenty years. It's actually closer to sixteen years, to be precise."

"So, 'boobies' is a thirteen-year-old-boy word?" I snickered again, not surprised at all. I'd been known to crack up over word choices for years. It was official. I had the mind of a thirteen-year-old boy.

After that, the conversation took on a hazy quality. I lost track of what my thirteen-year-old mind said, but I was pretty sure I asked Nathan to put his trunk in me again, which was what I was going for before the booze messed it up.

2. *The Big Head Versus the Little Head*

NATHAN

I couldn't help contemplating my actions that evening as I carried her motionless body into the small cottage in the woods. If lightning struck me at that moment, I could see where it was justified. The moment I entered the bar, I seemed to ignore every rule I'd ever set. My rules were simple enough that a fucking two-year-old could follow them. Find my target, evaluate the situation, contact the parties concerned, find my target, evaluate the situation, contact the parties . . . I never deviated from this routine for a reason. I had a job to do. A job I was good at. A job free from personal attachments. It was a routine that suited me well. Of course, the delicate brunette I held in my arms contradicted all of it.

I shifted her slightly in my arms, suppressing a chuckle as she let out a loud snore when her head rolled backward over my arm. I pulled her more securely against my chest as I carried her through the only doorway into the cottage. I didn't want to admit to myself how much time I'd invested that evening thinking about what she would feel like pressed against me. Of course, carrying her like this wasn't the kind of pressing I'd had in mind. Her delicate frame made it easy to shoulder her weight, and she had a firm body; I could feel that even through her clothes. It'd be embarrassing as fuck right now if she woke up and saw the hard-on I had just from holding her. Unable to resist, I inhaled her heady perfume one last time before gently placing her on the bed. For a brief crazy moment, I considered crawling into bed next to her. It had been years since I'd felt the urge to actually stay in a bed with a woman any longer than it took to have sex with her. You couldn't call it "making love" since it was never intimate enough for that. Hell, it wasn't even "fucking" since even that required emotion. It was just sex. Nothing but two bodies coming together to scratch an itch.

I backed away from the bed and left the room before I could cave to the urge. She was an assignment, not a means to scratch an itch. Besides, it was a dick move to mix business with pleasure, and a threshold I never crossed. It was time for me to leave anyway. I had made contact with my target, and by tomorrow my job would be done. Instead of heading for the front door, though, I walked to the far side of the room, where a small functional kitchen was located. I'm not sure why I bothered going to the trouble, but I filled a glass with water and palmed the bottle of aspirin off the top of the re-

frigerator where it was sandwiched between a bag of pow-
dered mini doughnuts and a stack of magazines. I focused on
remaining professional as I returned to the room where the
spitfire temptress was still snoring. Helping her through her
hangover would only make my job easier in the morning. It
would help expedite the job. Glancing down at her unconscious body, I decided I might as well make her as comfortable
as I could, so I set the water and aspirin on the nightstand and
got to work pulling off her jeans and shirt. *You're not a perv*,
I kept telling myself. *You're just trying to make her more comfortable*. Of course, tell that to the other particular part of my
body that was responding to her creamy smooth skin and
brutal curves. With one last reluctant look and an apology to
my painfully throbbing boys, I pulled the quilt over her and
exited the room.

I locked the cottage door behind me and headed purpose-
fully toward my trusty Range Rover before I could change my
mind and climb between the crisp sheets with her.

The drive back to my hotel was short, given the town's size.
Two stop signs after pulling off the dirt road that led to Ashton's small but charming cottage, I pulled into the parking lot
of the only hotel in town. It was actually more of a motel, but
I guess they figured slapping the title of *Hotel* onto the sign
made it more legitimate. As long as the room was clean and
the staff stayed out of my way, it suited my purposes. The last
thing I needed was for some nosy maid to riffle through my
papers and find out why I was really in town.

The hotel was cemetery quiet as I climbed out of the Range

Rover and locked it behind me. The late hour combined with the stillness around me provided a ghost-town-like aura. It felt strange to be out here in the middle of nowhere. Ever since I arrived here I'd been wondering why a rich girl like Ashton had picked this town to hide. I would have expected the glitzy lights of New York or the party atmosphere of Chicago to appeal to her, but instead she'd chosen Woodfalls. I'd seen her type over the years: rich, easily bored, with big-time diva complexes. Woodfalls was too tame for someone like that.

I pushed the motel room door open with my foot after sliding the key into the lock, making sure the *Do Not Disturb* sign remained on the door. Once I switched on the lights, Ashton's face greeted me from the multiple images hanging on the wall. Each image depicted her in a different setting and pose, all courtesy of my client. Studying the pictures of her smiling, I couldn't help noting how the images didn't do her eyes justice. They couldn't capture the same sparkle I had witnessed earlier that evening. Just remembering how she'd smiled at me with her bright shiny eyes made me want her even more.

"This is ridiculous," I thought, shaking my head in disgust. I backed up to the edge of my bed and sank down onto the sagging mattress. What the hell was I doing? Lusting after a target was unacceptable. I was hired to make contact, observe, and report back to my client. That was it. I wasn't hired to sniff at her ass like a dog in heat—no matter how appealing that might be.

Striding to the bathroom, I stripped off my clothes in

aggravation and cranked the shower to its coldest setting, hoping a cold shower would shock my system. Five minutes later, I stood with a towel around my waist, glaring at the traitor between my legs. It wasn't like I was sexually deprived. Something about Ashton just appealed to me. Well, not just something. It was everything. She was smoking hot.

My cell phone vibrated on the nightstand, pulling my mind from the gutter I couldn't seem to get out of. It was a little late for this call, but considering I'd neglected to check in today, I wasn't too surprised.

"Yes, sir," I answered.

"Did you find her?" the voice on the other end asked, offering up no greeting.

The words of affirmation were on the edge of my tongue, but I surprised myself by answering negatively. "Not yet, sir. I have a lead, though. It should only be a matter of time before I locate her."

"You gave the impression the last time we conversed that you were following a lead."

"It's the same lead," I lied. "It's only a matter of time before I pinpoint her location."

"The sooner, the better," he grumbled, hanging up without any further words.

I returned the phone to the nightstand and slid back against the pillows. That was unsettling. I'd never lied to a client before. For three weeks I'd been on Ashton's trail. I should have been happy to finally close up the case and head back to my condo in Tampa for some much-needed R&R. Just that morning I'd been dreaming about taking several months off to catch up on some fishing and scuba diving. This case was ready to be wrapped within twenty-four hours, but now, suddenly, I was dragging it out. All for her. From the moment I'd laid eyes on Ashton I'd been acting like a complete jackass, letting my little head outthink my big head. As soon as I'd walked in the bar tonight, I was taken in by her. I'd scanned the smoke-filled room, spotting her with her friends, joking and carrying on in the far corner. It was obvious the moment they noticed my presence because their voices came out in short bursts of excited chatter followed by whispering. I figured it was only a matter of time until I was approached. Bar scenes didn't get their hookup stigma for no reason. Eight years ago, it would have been my buddies and me in the far corner of the bar playing the game. All of us banking on getting laid that night. More times than not, we'd all gone home alone. We were young, dumb, testosterone-crazed maniacs that most chicks wouldn't touch with a ten-foot pole.

Then I met Jessica and fell head over heels in love with her. She was poised and polished and challenged me to be better. Jessica wasn't into the whole club scene, so I gave it up, without a fuss. My buddies were pissed, claiming I was pussywhipped, but I didn't care. What did I need the clubs for anymore? I'd found the perfect girl. A year later, I realized perfection was nothing but an illusion. She'd shredded me to the point where I swore I'd never let a woman have that power over me again. I jumped back into the bar scene a changed man. I couldn't have cared less about trying to get any girl's attention. Instead, I made them come to me. The guys thought I was crazy, but my aloof attitude worked better than any of the stupid one-liners or any other shit we used to do. I always laid my rules out in the open to avoid any future complications, and most of the time, the relationship would end amicably. Only one had called me a bastard, but I held steadfast to my rule. No attachments. Take it or leave it.

I'd kept my eyes on the trio in the corner through the mirror over the bar, waiting to see who would make the first move. I had several game plans in place. If I was approached by one of them, I would suggest buying a round for her and her friends so I could get close to my target. If they chickened out and never made their move, I'd order a round anyway and see if I could strike up a conversation that way. One thing was certain: I would not have walked away tonight without making contact.

It had taken fifteen minutes for the group of girls to finally make their move. Much to my astonishment, it was Ashton instead of her heavily endowed friend who approached me. After listening to her boisterous friend, I would have bet money that she would be my first contact with the group. The night was shaping up to be filled with surprises. My good fortune continued as Ashton awkwardly began to flirt with me. Seizing the opportunity, I ordered a round of drinks to see if that would loosen her tongue further. Much to my pleasure, the whiskey not only loosened her tongue, providing me with information, but it also provided a glimpse into something more. Her voice washed over me like a seductive caress, laced with an equal share of innocence and wisdom that hinted at a hidden inner pain. Something was bothering her, but regardless, whatever it was didn't concern me. It wasn't my job to rescue her. She was just an assignment, nothing more.

With each round of drinks, though, that fact continued to dissipate. The more she talked, the more I was pulled in. Even her fumbled attempt at sexual banter was endearing and erotic at the same time. When she asked if I wanted to put my trunk in her, I got rock hard and wanted to hoist her up on the counter and take her right there in front of everyone.

I reached over for my cell phone to check the time and was shocked when I realized I had been lying there thinking about her for the past hour. I reached over and flipped the light switch, plunging the room into darkness. As I contemplated my next move, the sane part of me knew I should call my client first thing in the morning and hand over Ashton's location, but the slightly insane side considered the possibility of waiting a few days to see if I could flush out why she had run away. The irrationality of this thought wasn't lost on me. It shouldn't matter why she'd run off. I was paid to locate her, plain and simple. It wasn't my business to ask questions. The fact that I had the sudden urge to hunt down my client instead and bury my fist in his face for ever hurting her shook me to the core. It had been years since a woman had had this effect on me.

Insanity. That was all it was. I would turn her in tomorrow. It was the only way to get my mind back on track. I'd had no problems keeping the women I dated at arm's length for the last seven years. I wasn't about to screw that up over some girl I'd been tracking for the past three weeks.

3. *What Happened Last Night?*

ASHTON

My head felt like I was in hell with a herd of elephants in tap shoes. Dragging the pillow off my head, I looked around to find my room empty, but someone was insistently pounding on the front door.

"Oh, mother of all things holy, shut up, and stop the god-damn pounding," I squawked out as I attempted to sit up. The sound of my own voice made me cringe and want to curl up into a ball as needles of pain shot through my head. Stumbling to my feet, I grabbed the pair of yoga pants and T-shirt I'd left draped over the foot of my bed the previous day. I nearly fell over trying to pull them on before I shuffled my way to the front door of my rental cottage. I threw open the door, ready to poke the eyes out of the offending knockers.

"Took you long enough. You were supposed to text us, you

bitch. We were worried sick," Tressa yelled, making me cover my ears in agony as my eyes watered in pain. My stomach flipped, making its own displeasure glaringly obvious. Lurching past my two astonished friends, I stumbled to the bushes that bordered the front of my cottage and expelled all the liquor I'd consumed the previous evening. My stomach muscles clenched as I continued to heave even after there was nothing left to come out. Ironically, the last time this happened, I swore I'd never puke again. The waves of nausea were not foreign to me. I had spent more time kneeling before a toilet puking than I liked to think about. Of course, those circumstances were different, and the poisons in my bloodstream at that time were worlds apart. If this was what resulted from a night of drinking, I was out.

"Holy shit, that's a lot of puke," Tressa said behind me as Brittni handed me a cold rag to mop up my face. "I think you might have drunk a little too much," she said.

"Oh, you think, ole wise one?" I sniped. "Can we use our indoor voices?" I asked, holding a finger in front of my lips for emphasis.

"You have a headache?" Tressa asked, snickering behind me as I stumbled back into my cottage and sank down on the couch.

"A headache I could handle. This is a freaking jackhammer," I mumbled, letting my head fall back against the cushions of the couch. "Please tell me why I drank so many shots?" I moaned.

"More importantly, how was the sex?" Tressa interrupted impatiently.

My eyes flew open at her words. Stumbling to my feet, I dashed to my bedroom, sweeping my eyes around to see if I'd missed his presence in my mad bolt out of the room earlier.

"Are you expecting him to crawl out from under the bed, or maybe jump out of your wardrobe?" Brittni asked dryly, peering over my shoulder at the large wardrobe that served as the only closet in the whole cottage. I had cringed at first when I walked through the place before renting it and realized there were no closets. How anyone could function without closets was beyond me, but the charm of the cottage had overlapped the lack of storage space, and I'd managed to make it work.

"You're a riot," I replied, sinking down on my bed.

"So, did Tall, Dark, and Sexy do the old bang-and-bolt?" Tressa asked, surveying my room critically.

"Um, I don't know. I can't remember," I admitted, mortified. How much did I drink that I couldn't even remember whether I'd had sex?

"You mean, you don't remember him leaving, or you don't remember banging, Bang-a-licious?"

"Either," I answered weakly, cupping my throbbing head in my hands while fighting a fresh onslaught of nausea. It was official. I was a slut. Not only did I pick up strange men in a bar, but I also had sex with them without remembering it.

"What's the last thing you remember?" Brittni asked, sinking down on the other side of me.

"I remember talking with you guys in the bathroom and then joining him. I also remember talking to him . . . Oh God," I squawked.

"What?" Tressa demanded.

"I'm pretty sure I asked him if he was going to put his trunk in my head, or his trunk in me or something," I mumbled through my fingers.

"What?" Tressa busted out before laughing. "Well, that's one way to tell him you're interested," she gasped.

"I didn't mean it. The whiskey had my tongue all tied together. I meant to ask him if he was going to put my head in his trunk. And stop laughing. It's not that funny," I grumbled as Brittni joined in her laughter.

"Oh my God, that's classic. How did he respond?"

"How do you think?" I said, peeking through my fingers, which covered my face.

"Okay, so you asked him to put his trunk in you," she snorted, trying to choke down her laughter. "What else?"

"Well, after that it gets kind of hazy. I know he ordered more rounds and at one point I believe I may have suggested strip darts. God, kill me now."

"Wow, you went all out," Tressa quipped, laughing again. "So, how far did the game of darts go?"

"I have no idea. I can't remember fuck-all after that. For all I know, I probably ran around Joe's buck naked."

"If you had, my mom would have been on it like white on rice, and it wasn't included in her daily scandal rap sheet, so I'd say you're safe," Brittni reassured me, grinning wickedly. "Were you wearing that when you woke up?" she asked, pointing to the clothes I'd pulled on.

"No, I was wearing my bra and panties," I answered, looking down at the T-shirt, which was on backward.

"Hmmm, I find it hard to believe he'd bother to put your bra and panties on after ravishing your body, so chances are you passed out on Prince Hotness. Judging by the glass of water and bottle of aspirin on your table, he's part Prince Charming too," Brittni observed, pointing to my nightstand. "Here, take these," she said, popping open the bottle of aspirin. "Maybe you can just ask him where he put his trunk the next time you see him," she added, laughing.

"I can't, he was just passing through. He's some kind of journalist and was on his way to his next story," I said, tossing back the pills before lying back on my bed. "So, you don't think I slept with him?" I asked, not sure if I was relieved. Sure, I wanted to get that one item marked off my list, but I kind of felt like it was cheating if I didn't remember it.

"I don't know. What do you feel like down there?" Tressa asked.

"What do you mean?" I asked, wary of where this was going.

"I mean, are things messy down there?" she replied, pointing between my legs.

"Oh, Jesus, Tressa, come on," Brittni piped in.

"Okay, I'm just kidding. I'm guessing he did not stick his trunk in your head or any other orifice on your body," Tressa confirmed, snickering again.

"Laugh it up. Karma's a bitch," I mumbled, throwing my arms over my eyes in a halfhearted attempt to block out the sunlight streaming through the sheer curtains over the bay window in the room.

"Don't you have to work today?" Brittni asked, straightening up my bed around me.

"Yeah, but not till noon," I said as the lull of sleep pulled me toward it.

"I don't know how to break it to you, sweets, but it's eleven fifteen," she pointed out.

"What the hell? Are you kidding?" I bolted upright in my bed, peering at my clock in dismay. "How did it get so late?" I said, jumping to my feet and racing toward my bathroom.

"Why do you think we were freaking out when we didn't hear from you? By ten thirty I was ready to call in the cavalry, but Brittni convinced me the sane thing would be to check on you first. Didn't your phone go off from all the messages we sent you?"

"Frick, I'm not even sure where my purse is," I said, scanning the room for my purse. "Maybe Nathan only pretended to be interested so he could rob me blind while I was drunk and passed out. 'Nathan' probably wasn't even his real name."

"Chillax, girl. Your purse is on your chair," Brittni said, striding toward the chair to pick up my purse. "Your phone is here, but it's as dead as the roadkill Creepy Freddy likes to eat," she added, holding up my phone.

"Damn, I better charge it," I said, glancing at my clock again.

"Go shower and we'll plug it in for you," Tressa said, shooing me toward the bathroom. "Text us after you get off work," she called out as I closed the bathroom door behind me.

Thirty minutes later I pulled into the dusty side lot of Smith's General Store. When I had first arrived in town four months ago, I knew I wanted to work here. Not because I had some deep desire to stock shelves or bag groceries, but because it was a blast from another time. When I was thirteen, I was obsessed with the TV show *Gilmore Girls*. The show was about a young single mother raising her teenage daughter, and although the show delved into deep issues occasionally, it was the quirkiness of the small town that pulled me in. I'm sure some psychologist could have a field day comparing my attachment to the show with the loss of my mom. That was probably part of it, but after living in an overly populated city in Florida all my life, I'd always yearned for a small town. A town where friendships went deeper than just acquaintances you went to school with. I wanted friendships that couldn't be shaken, no matter what obstacles might get in the way. I wanted a town where if you got sick, people actually cared. Maybe they would even care enough to check up on you, or bombard you with soups and casseroles, or who knows what. The point is, they wouldn't shun you, or refuse to come near you because they thought they might catch something. Before I arrived in Woodfalls, I thought a town like that only existed on TV, but so far this place has lived up to my expectations. Woodfalls was charming and quirky and certainly not perfect, but that just made it even better. I fell in love instantly and was able to cross yet another item off my bucket list.

"You look like something even the cat wouldn't want to drag in," Fran greeted me as I entered the store.

"Well, I feel like something even the dog wouldn't want to bury," I replied, grabbing an apron off the hook behind the old-fashioned counter where a dated cash register sat. Not that we actually used it; Fran kept it for nostalgia reasons. Even in sleepy Woodfalls, we actually had computerized registers.

"Rough night?" she asked with double meaning, eyeing me critically. Fran was the only person who knew why I was really here. I felt it was only fair to tell her the truth, since one day I might just disappear again. For all her feistiness, she is still a sweet lady. If she had concerns about me working here, she never let it show, and has always paid me under the table to keep me off the books. It was just a safety precaution because I wasn't sure if anyone would ever come looking for me. Truthfully, I really didn't even need to work. I had a trust fund that had been turned over to me the day I turned twenty-one. The days leading up to my disappearance, I'd gone to the bank each day and withdrawn the allotted amount that wouldn't raise a red flag. My window of opportunity was short, though, because once the monthly statement came in, the jig would be up. By the time that happened, I was long gone with enough liquid cash to keep me comfortable.

"Not like you think," I answered, unpacking a box of candy bars. "I went out with Tressa and Brittni," I added as explanation for my hungover appearance.

"Ah, I see," she said chuckling. "Tipped up a few too many, did ya?"

"A few I could have handled. The dozen or so after that is what killed me," I said, grimacing at the memory of my puke party earlier. If I never drank whiskey again, it would be too soon. "But at least I can cross getting trashed off my list."

"I don't remember getting trashed being on your list," she chirped, hoisting up a heavy box of canned goods before depositing them in front of the shelf where they needed to be unpacked.

"Oh, it wasn't, but after the pain I felt this morning, it was a last-minute write-in because I'm never going there again," I said, coming around the counter to help her carry the heavy boxes to the appropriate aisles. "I told you to stop lugging those heavy boxes around. That's why you hired me, right?" I chastised.

"Oh, sugar, I've been lugging boxes around before you were ever thought of. I hired you so I'd stop being the crazy old woman who talks to herself all day."

"You're so full of it. I know for a fact that Mr. James from the hardware store comes in here daily just to see you."

"He just likes the jerky I keep in stock." She smirked, pulling a box cutter out of the pocket of her apron and carefully slicing the clear tape that sealed the carton.

"I believe you. Not. He comes in here because he wants to ride the Fran train," I retorted, tongue-in-cheek.

"Bite your tongue, young lady," Fran admonished me. She acted scandalized, but I knew better. Fran was a reality TV junkie, especially *The Real Housewives*. She claimed they were better than soap operas any day. "I should wash your mouth out," she threatened.

"Don't deny it. I've seen the way he checks you out when

he's here. Just like I've seen you admiring his backside," I added, wagging my eyebrows at her.

"Honey, at our age, our asses are either bony as hell or a saggy mess of flesh. There's a reason our eyesight goes the older we get."

I snorted with laughter at her bluntness. That was why I enjoyed working with her so much; she always kept it real.

The tinkling of the bell over the door stalled any further comments. Fran shuffled off to the stockroom to deposit the empty boxes while I continued stocking the shelves. I could hear the customer in the next aisle and didn't bother to look up, figuring it was Mr. James to see Fran again. A moment later, though, a shadow fell over me and I stiffened momentarily when the heavy cologne the individual was wearing swirled around me. It was a scent that was already imprinted in my memory bank. I whirled around with dread, knowing exactly who towered over me. My precarious stance and the fact that my head wasn't a hundred percent back to normal worked against me as I lost my balance and landed hard on my butt. The momentum of my fall sent me crashing into the pyramid of cans I had just assembled, making them fly in every direction.

"Well, shit," I grumbled when I found myself flat on my ass at his feet. Would there be no end to embarrassing myself in front of him?

"Here, let me help you up," he said chivalrously, in the same sexy voice from the night before. If I'd had any thoughts that his voice only sounded sinful then because of the amount of alcohol I had consumed, I was delusional.

"I got it," I said, hoisting myself up with as much dignity as I could summon. Once I got myself upright, I finally spared a glance at him. To my dismay, he was studying me in the same bemused manner as the previous evening. Without whiskey clouding my brain, I didn't find it as cute to be the object of his amusement. "What are you doing here?" I sniped.

"Is the store closed?" he asked, looking around.

"Not 'in the store, here.' I mean, what are you still doing in town? I thought you were just passing through."

"Disappointed?" he asked. "I decided after our engaging conversation last night that maybe I'd check out all the perks you mentioned of living in a small town. You made it all seem so appealing, so I thought, 'Hey, I gotta be missing out.' I thought I could make it into a story. You know, a whole expo on small-town life and the dynamics that pull a community together, something like that. It dragged you here, so there has to be some kind of story."

Well, hell. He was sticking around because of my blabbermouth. I'd say I'd officially had the worst one-night stand ever. Not only did I pass out before the grand finale, I'd also convinced him to stay, taking away the anonymity of the whole one-night thing. If the floor opened up and sucked me in at that moment, it would have been more welcome than facing my failure in front of me.

"Are you okay?" he asked, grasping my elbow as if to steady me.

"Absolutely. Why?" I asked, extracting my elbow from his grasp.

"You looked kind of green there for a second."

"I guess I was just surprised to see you again after last night . . ." I said, letting my voice trail.

"Ah, yes. Last night was epic, unlike any other. Definitely eye-opening and educational. Who knew darts could be so much fun?" he remarked.

"Damn, we did play darts?" I asked, sagging weakly against the shelf behind me and knocking several cans over in the process.

"You got something against cans?" he asked, bending over to pick up the mess.

"We played darts?" I repeated, unwilling to move on. The thought of stripping my clothes off in front of everyone at the bar made my blood run cold, especially here in Woodfalls.

"Well, 'play' would be stretching it. You were too busy taking your clothes off to play darts."

"Holy shit, kill me now," I said, covering my face with my hands. "Are you telling me Joe and Mr. Jones saw me naked?"

"Was Mr. Jones the grumpy guy a couple tables from where you and your friends were sitting?"

"Yes," I said weakly, feeling sick all over again. There was no way this would stay a secret. Brittni might have joked about her mom's knack for sniffing out gossip, but it was closer to the truth than not. Once she got wind of it, the story would be bounced around until every resident in Woodfalls had heard about it.

"Then, no, neither of them saw you naked," he said, grinning wickedly.

"What?" I squawked out, not sure I heard him right.

"I said, 'Neither of them saw your boobies,'" he answered, reminding me of yet another embarrassing aspect from the night before. I'd completely forgotten about the whole boobies conversation.

"I'm not ordinarily like that," I clarified.

"Oddly enough, you mentioned that several times last night, among other things."

"You know, it's really not very gentlemanly to remind a lady of a bad night," I sniped.

"I never said I was a gentleman," he replied, turning on his heel to leave.

"Wait, what about, um . . . did we . . . you know," I stumbled out, loathing the fact that I had to ask.

"You mean did we make wild, passionate love all night?" he asked, turning back around and walking toward me.

"Uh, yeah," I whispered as my pulse stuttered before kicking into hyperspeed as I hung on his answer.

"You don't remember my hands all over your body, or the way you moaned when I kissed you here?" he asked, seductively caressing my neck.

All I could do was shake my head. I dragged my bottom lip into my mouth and gnawed on it before abruptly releasing it. His eyes darkened as they settled on my now-damp lips.

"Or here?" he asked, stroking his thumb across my bottom lip.

My body responded instantly to his touch. Biting back a moan, I looked up at him expectantly, willing him to remind me what his lips had felt like on mine.

My breath came out in short pants as he leaned in close and grazed his lips over my ear. "Too bad you passed out before we could do anything," he whispered. "Maybe one of these days we'll both get to see what it feels like," he added, nipping my earlobe before abruptly turning and walking away.

Just like that, I was a puddle of lust. All my embarrassment from the night before disappeared in the blink of an eye only to be replaced with regret. I wanted to wrap myself around his chiseled body and pull him tightly between my legs. Never in my whole life had I ever reacted so radically to someone. I felt like a cat in heat, or at the very least, a horny teenage boy.

It took a few seconds for reason to finally make an appearance. "Get a grip," I finally muttered to myself when I realized I was still watching him. "Sure, he was hot, but seriously, there was nothing special about him," I lied as I distracted myself by restacking the pyramid of cans I had knocked over. The fact that Nathan had decided to stick around nixed any plans of us ever hooking up. I was only looking for a one-night stand, not a relationship, and definitely nothing that would lead to any sort of attachment. My indulgence the night before had cost me maybe the hottest night in bed I would ever have, but it wasn't like I could rewind time.

4. *The Decision*

NATHAN

Going to the store had been a mistake. I'd woken up this morning with the plan to call the client, but as I was showering, I couldn't shake Ashton's image from my mind. Against my better judgment, I decided to head to the small store where she worked. There was no reason to go. I had all the information I needed to end the case. I just wanted to get a glimpse of her one last time before I walked away. It was a purely selfish move, but I figured no one would get hurt. My client would have to wait a little longer for Ashton's location, but a few hours never killed anyone.

Feeling jittery from my decision to put off the call, I decided to walk to the store rather than drive to clear my mind. The air outside had a crispness that wouldn't be felt in Florida until mid-December. It was actually a pleasure to walk outside without sweating my ass off from humidity, and had me contemplating whether I should hang up my scuba gear and head north. I'd miss diving, but the trade-off might be worth it. I'd lived in the same city in Florida all my life, and only stayed out of habit. When I was younger, I had lived in a small one-story house with my parents, though I don't really remember it. The summer I turned seven, my asshole father flipped my life upside down when he decided he liked nailing his secretary better than living with us. My mom was too proud and hurt over his betrayal to take his money. The bills had piled up, and eventually we were forced to leave the house behind. My grandparents welcomed us into their house, but it was way too small, even for four people. It was only for a short time anyway, while my mom scrimped and saved every cent she could. A small inheritance from a distant aunt added to our nest egg and finally, she was able to buy a single-wide trailer for us to live in. I was young enough to find the move to the trailer park exciting and different than our old neighborhood, which was mostly made up of grouchy elderly couples. There were plenty of kids to play with, and during the summer, the trailer park opened the community pool. I was in hog heaven. It would be years later that I would realize how hard it had been on my mom to lose our house.

Living in a trailer did have its downfalls. It seemed every time we turned around something needed to be repaired. The repairs always seemed to set Mom's teeth on edge, but it was the Florida storms that worried her the most. During hurricane season she would watch the TV incessantly all hours of the night any time there was a storm brewing over the ocean. When I was ten, I asked her why we lived in a trailer and not a house if storms worried her so much. Her eyes had filled with tears before she swallowed hard and sat me down.

"I bought this trailer because that's all the money I had. I wanted something that was ours. No one will ever be able to take this from us. We will never be without a home again," she'd told me with steel in her voice. At that moment, I hated my lying-sack-of-shit father more than anything. He'd taken away the one thing that meant the most to her. I swore at that moment I would one day buy her a house just like the one she had lost. That day never came. She died three weeks before my twenty-third birthday. Not long after Jessica had torn my world to shreds. Within days, I had lost the two women I had loved—one from betrayal and the other from the irresponsible teenager who decided to run a red light.

I pushed the memories back to the far recesses of my mind. Now was not the time to get sentimental over memories that were best forgotten. I didn't want to remember how my mom had worked herself to the bone to provide for me, too proud to ever take money from my prick of a father.

By the time I made it to the general store, my past was locked away in the vault where it belonged. One solitary car sat forlorn in the dusty lot when I reached the store. I recognized it instantly as the one that had been parked in front of

Ashton's cottage when I dropped her off the night before. Pushing the door open, I convinced myself that seeing her one last time would give me the closure I needed before reporting her whereabouts.

Of course, the little head took over again and rose to the occasion as soon as I laid eyes on Ashton bent over, stacking cans. My eyes traced the rounded curves of her ass and down a pair of perfectly sculpted legs. I wanted nothing more than to put my hands on her hips and pull her flush against the part of me that was hard with arousal. When I left the store fifteen minutes later, I was in physical pain. I couldn't remember a time I'd ever wanted a woman as much as I wanted her. She was every bit as enticing as she'd been the night before, if not more so. Without the alcohol to loosen her up, she had blushed as red as a sunburn when I had teased her about her memory lapse from the previous evening. I could have stood there all day talking to her, but eventually, what had started as playful banter had escalated to downright lust. Dragging her delicate earlobe into my mouth was almost my undoing, and I had to force myself to walk away from her before I hauled her up in my arms and took what she'd offered so willingly the night before.

It took the entire walk back to the hotel for everything she instigated in my body to return to normal. Once my mind was able to focus on something other than what it would feel like sliding into her, I made a decision: Forget my rules this time and make her mine. We would do the deed once and the hunger would be abated. The magnetic pull she had over me would disappear, and I would complete the job I was hired for. I just needed to work her out of my system; then I'd turn her over and she would cease to be my concern after that. I felt more in control once I had the plan worked out in my head, despite the small voice that told me I was full of shit.

5. *Free Fall*

ASHTON

"Gettin' pretty friendly with the customers there," Fran teased after Nathan finally strolled out of the store, seemingly unaffected by the fact that I was practically in a liquid state from his actions.

"I met him last night," I admitted, sure that it wouldn't take her long to connect the dots.

"I see. Well, honey darling, I'm thinking you two missed the page on one-night stands," she said with laughing eyes as she settled on the stool behind the counter.

"We didn't even make it to 'one-night stand' status. I passed out before we could even do the deed, which means that item is still on my list," I complained, placing my elbows on the counter so I could rest my chin on my hands. "I was an idiot to add that to my list."

"You're not an idiot. You're just someone trying to forget a tough past. I don't condone jumping in bed with a stranger, but I also know that every woman deserves the right to have at least one night where a man loves her right. You deserve that toe-curling experience, honey darling, and judging by the looks of it, Mr. Sexy Voice would be very accommodating in that category."

"But it's too late for that. I can't have a one-night stand with someone I could bump into the next day. That defeats the whole purpose. Hot sex with no attachments, remember?"

"Honey, with a man like that, one night wouldn't do you anyway. I saw the way he was looking at you."

"It's a moot point," I sighed. "I'm not looking for a relationship."

"I know you're not, sugar, but there's no reason you can't allow yourself to live a little," she said, nudging me toward the stool she had been using. I smiled grimly at her observation. She'd come to know me well in a short period of time and was able to tell I was exhausted without me saying a word.

"I'm pretty sure someone your age should be telling me I should wait until marriage or something like that," I said dryly as I sank down on the stool.

She snorted loudly. "Sugar, I've never given the traditional advice. It's probably my words of wisdom that sent my poor Earl to an early grave. That poor dear never knew what was going to come out of my mouth. I drove that boy to insanity with my naughty mouth when he was courting me. His parents nearly stroked out the first time he brought me home. I'm pretty sure his prissy mom told him to drop me immediately before I tainted their family blood. Earl wouldn't hear of it. I had him snagged hook, line, and sinker. He proposed three months after our first date and we were married two months after that. He later admitted he couldn't have waited another moment to have me. Turns out, my naughty talking had him in a sexual tizzy the entire time we were dating," she said, chuckling at the memory. "His momma wore black to the wedding."

"You minx," I teased. She joked about it, but it was obvious she missed her husband greatly even though he'd been gone for fifteen years. I envied their love story, knowing something like that wasn't in my cards.

"You're no different than me, young lady. I saw how that tall drink of handsomeness was looking at you. He looks at you like my Earl used to look at me. You mark my words: He wants you like a condemned man yearns for freedom."

"Are you giving me permission to have an affair?" I joked, using the duster that was stowed under the counter to dust around where I was sitting, so I was at least being a little productive.

"I'm telling you, you deserve to live a little," she said, giving me a one-armed hug before heading back to her office in the stockroom.

Contemplating her words, I pulled out my purse from beneath the cabinet. I rifled through it until I found the sheet of paper I was looking for. I smoothed it out on the counter and read over the long list. There were twenty-seven things listed on the paper, and only fifteen of them were crossed out. I realized I wouldn't be able to finish everything on the list before time ran out. My days in Woodfalls were numbered. Soon I would have to face the music and return to my old life. Maybe Fran was right. The list wasn't written in stone. One item could easily be switched out for another. I gnawed indecisively on my thumbnail for a moment before I finally grabbed a pen out of the cup by the register. With shaking fingers, I crossed out *One-Night Stand with a Stranger* and wrote in *Have an Affair with Sexy-Voice Nathan*. This was insane. How did I go from *one night* to *affair*? When did I become this bold person? I knew exactly when I became that kind of person: It was the day I learned that life was short and you needed to seize the opportunity to live.

The rest of the afternoon passed quickly as Fran and I continued to stock the shelves. A steady stream of customers came in, mostly to buy items they'd forgotten in their weekly or monthly grocery shopping trip at the large store by the highway. Each of them would spend a few minutes looking for their items and then another ten chatting with Fran and me if I was around. It was the way it worked around here. Most of the conversation was gossip, and as fate would have it, I was the main topic. It seemed word had gotten out that I had drunk enough to float a battleship with a complete stranger. Thanks to Joe's big mouth, everyone knew about my disastrous evening. At first, I was mortified that all three thousand residents probably knew that I'd been out flirting with some guy I didn't even know, but by the fourth customer, I reminded myself that this was the reason I moved here. I wanted that small-town feel, the good and the bad. Fran was a godsend throughout the afternoon. When the ribbing got too personal, she'd remind the patrons of any past deeds they weren't too proud of. It seemed like she had dirt on everyone. It was a benefit of being that old and living here as long as she had. She'd seen a lot of people grow from child to adult in this town and witnessed many things people would now like to forget.

I was still chuckling after she reminded busybody Chrissy Dean about the time she got caught with Michael Ridge's hand up her skirt during the homecoming dance back in '99. Chrissy scurried off, mumbling about people having the memory of an elephant.

"Fran, how do you know all this crap?" I asked, locking the door and flipping the *Closed* sign over.

"Darling, I realized years ago that in a town this size you need to keep track of things. When a scandal arises, everyone suddenly forgets their own past sins. After seeing a couple of the newer residents run off by gossip years ago, I decided to make it my job to remind everyone that no one is perfect. Could you imagine how boring it would be if we were?" she asked, shuddering as she flipped off the light switch, plunging the store into semidarkness.

"At your age, shouldn't you be walking the straight and narrow?" I asked, heading out the back door with her. The question was meant to tease, but there was a layer of curiosity beneath it. What happened to us after we died was a nagging question in my head. Even though I knew some would say my curiosity was morbid.

"Honey, it's too late for me. I figure, either God will give me a free pass for my charming personality, or he'll give me the boot. It's too late to be fixin' things now."

"Heaven would be lucky to have you," I said loyally, walking down the cobblestone path with her.

"You know, honey, you don't need to walk me home," she reminded me, the same way she did every night. "My house is less than two hundred yards from the store, not two miles," she added.

"I like walking you home, so there," I told her, not mentioning the fact that it made me feel better to keep an eye on her while she navigated the uneven path in the dark. I knew it would piss her off if I admitted I was afraid she'd trip or something. I knew how much her independence meant to her.

"Do you want to stay for dinner?" she asked, opening her front door, which was never locked.

"Not tonight. I think I'm going to hit the sack early."

"Any big plans tomorrow?"

"Well, since it's Sunday, and we're closed, I'm going to cross another item off my list. I need to kick it into high gear if I'm going to finish all the items," I said with a slight edge of panic in my voice.

"You'll do it. Which one are you doing?" she asked, although I could tell she already knew.

"The fear one," I answered, making busywork of searching for my car keys in my purse.

She clucked her tongue disapprovingly. It was the one item on my list she didn't approve of. She could handle the one-night stand or her suggestion of an affair, but conquering my fear of heights was a different story.

"You know I need to do it," I reminded her.

"There's plenty of ways to conquer that fear without jumping off some damn bridge. I'm sure your twins are all in," she retorted, referring to Tressa and Brittni.

"Brittni is. Tressa is deathly afraid of heights and claims she has no desire to ever conquer her fear."

"She's a smart girl."

"You didn't think that when she pranked Shelly last week, even though she is your least favorite customer," I threw out, finally finding my keys.

"Well, that's because sometimes that Tressa acts like she's still in high school. Besides, anyone with a brain knows it's not the best idea to wrap a store toilet bowl with Saran Wrap. Most people who use our bathroom really got to go, and having their pee puddled in their shoes is not good. I could not for the life of me figure out why there were wet footprints trailing from the bathroom door."

"It was gross," I laughed. "But you have to admit it was pretty funny how Shelly, scurried out of the store thinking she had missed the toilet."

"That was the only highlight of the whole incident," Fran replied, chuckling along with me. "I swear, that woman acts like being a minister's wife gives her the right to judge everyone else."

"Exactly, which is why Tressa hatched the idea."

"So, you're telling me Shelly was the target all along?" she asked, quirking her eyebrow at me.

"Um, yeah," I stammered, knowing I'd just given away my part in the prank.

"And how did dear Tressa know that Shelly would be the one to use the toilet?"

"I might have told her. Come on, you have to admit, her catty remarks every time she uses the bathroom get old.

"How did you know it would be her who got pranked?"

"Because she comes in every week after her ladies' tea . . ." My voice trailed off as I backed away from the door before I could implicate myself further. "I'll see you on Monday," I called over my shoulder, hurrying down the path.

"I knew you were involved," she called after me before closing her front door.

I laughed at her words as I approached my car. I threw my purse over on the passenger seat and climbed in behind the steering wheel. I was backing up my car when some kind of movement off to my right startled me. Whipping my head around, I saw a lone runner making his way down Main Street. Woodfalls had its share of walkers, but there really weren't any runners, and definitely not any like the one who was currently crossing the street in front of me. Ordinarily, I would have scoffed at a man running without a shirt on, wondering what he was trying to prove. Nathan, though, was a different story with his glistening pecs and rock-hard abs. It would have been sinful to deprive the female population of the opportunity to gawk. I sat motionless in my seat, watching as he ran by my car window. My heart thundered in my chest as I watched a trickle of sweat track its way down the deep contours of his well-muscled back, disappearing inside his shorts. He was long gone by the time I shook myself out of my fawning comatose state enough to drive home. I felt feverish. Glancing in the mirror, I saw that my face was flushed.

"God, you're a mess. What are you going to do if you ever see him naked? Spontaneously combust?" I asked my reflection.

The ringing of my cell phone woke me the next morning. I fumbled around my nightstand trying to find it while still keeping my eyes shut.

"Yeah," I croaked into the phone, my voice still heavy with sleep.

"Are you sick too?" Brittni's voice croaked back at me, although she sounded much worse.

"No, I was just sleeping. You're sick?" I asked the obvious. Either she was sick or she'd swallowed a very old frog.

"Yeah, my mom made Dr. Baker come out and check me. He said it looked like strep to him. I bet I got it from my damn students," she complained. Brittni subbed at the elementary school while she worked on getting her teaching degree. I found it ironic that she insisted she wanted to be a schoolteacher but didn't seem to like kids all that much. Tressa told me the dislike thing was actually an act. "She may be gruff, but she has mad skills when it comes to teaching," she had stated.

"Well, crap. I'm sorry you feel crummy," I offered, trying to hide my disappointment that I wouldn't be able to cross an item off my list.

"I'm sorry I'm bailing on you."

"It's no biggie. Just get better," I reassured her.

"Okay. We'll go when I get back from that stinking training thing next week," she promised before hanging up the phone.

I sat up, contemplating my list in my head to see if I could tackle one of the other items. I'd come from hot-as-hell Florida, so most of the items on my list centered on winter-related activities, with the obvious exception of the activity that possibly involved Nathan. A mental picture of a shirtless Nathan flashed through my head, making me jump out of bed abruptly. There was no way I was going to mope around all day. It was bad enough that thoughts of him had kept me up tossing and turning half the night.

I made my bed hastily and threw on a pair of cutoff shorts and T-shirt with a hooded sweatshirt over it. Ten minutes after hanging up the phone with Brittni, I was headed for Mason Bridge over on the county line. The air had a nip to it, making it clear that summer was over and fall was right around the corner. It felt glorious knowing it was September and already cooling off. In Florida, it would be several months before they saw similar temperatures. After a lifetime of missing real seasons, I was greedy for them to begin. I wanted to see the barren trees once they shed all their current multicolored leaves. I wanted to make a snow angel and build a snowman. All three were items on my bucket list that would take little effort as long as I was still here. I just needed enough time.

I was at Mason Bridge in less than five minutes. By the time I pulled off the side of the road just before the bridge, the nerves I'd been keeping at bay reared their ugly head. Sitting behind the steering wheel, I swiped my hands down my shorts in an attempt to remove the moisture that had collected on my palms. I could do this. Opening my car door, I forced myself to get out before I could chicken out and go home. The cool breeze blowing through the branches of the aged oak trees that lined the banks of the river below made me shiver slightly. I warily eyed the bridge in front of me. It was now or never. I stripped off my sweatshirt despite the chill and tossed it on the passenger seat next to the towel I had brought along. Closing the door with determination, I left my car behind, heading for the bridge.

My knees shook more and more the closer I got to the middle of the bridge, and my breath came out in labored puffs like I'd just sprinted a mile. Peering over the railing, I took in the slow-moving river below. From this height, the water looked darker and more menacing than I thought it would. I felt light-headed and slightly squeamish at the idea of being in water with God knows what lurking around me. In Florida, it was common knowledge that any body of water could have snakes or even gators. Indecision filled me as I gripped the railing with white knuckles. I clamped my eyes tightly closed to ward off the dizziness and gave myself a stern talking-to. I had to do it today. It was obvious by the chill in the air that time was limited. Pretty soon it would be too cold to jump.

With my mind made up, I kept my eyes closed as I attempted to climb over the railing, which I was still gripping with both hands. Maneuvering was awkward with the death grip I had, but after a few false starts, I was standing on the other side of the rail. Finally opening my eyes, I slowly released one hand so I could twist around to face the water below. With the railing against my back, I faced my biggest fear. My breath wheezed past my lips as I fought back my panic. "This is the worst part," I told myself. If I could get past this, the actual fall would last only seconds. Stiffening my back, I finally released the railing and moved to the edge of the bridge. The desire to slam my eyes shut again pulled at me, but I fought it back. There was no cheating this situation. With one last look of yearning at the railing behind me, I stepped off the bridge and screamed and screamed and then screamed some more.

My screams filled the air around me as I plunged toward the dark water below. It took less than a moment, and even though I was still scared, my screams were suddenly more exhilarated. I felt alive as my stomach dropped from the free fall. For the first time, I totally understood why skydivers claimed it was a rush like no other to jump out of a plane. I found I was actually disappointed when I hit the water feetfirst and sank down into the icy water. I wanted more. I wanted to feel the freedom of the fall all over again.

6. *Trying to Be the Hero*

NATHAN

I was three miles into my run on Sunday, contemplating my next move with Ashton, when I came across her car on the side of the road near Mason Bridge. Before I could register why it was there, a piercing scream rang through the air. Sprinting toward the location of the screams, I made it to the railing of the bridge just in time to see the splash of someone's body hitting the water below. Without giving it a thought, I hurled over the railing and jumped off the side of the bridge.

The water hit me like needles of ice as I was completely submerged. Years of scuba diving had me instinctively kicking my feet as I used my arms to propel me back to the surface. I swiped my hands frantically across my face, clearing away the water to look for her. Relief filled me as I saw a head bobbing in the water a few yards from me.

"What the hell? You scared the shit out of me!" Ashton yelled. "I thought the bridge was falling on me or something."

"Well, I thought you were being murdered by the way you were screaming," I countered, my own anger rising. "What the fuck are you doing?"

"I was conquering my fear of heights, quickly followed by my fear of a bridge falling on top of me," she sniped back, turning toward the shore. I watched for a moment as she used practiced strokes to propel herself toward the shore. Shaking my head in bewilderment, I followed behind, quickly catching up to her. We trudged the rest of the way to the shore once we could stand. Neither of us talked as the last of the adrenaline left us and our bodies began to shake from the cold. The tension between us dissipated when I reached out to steady her when she tripped over a hidden root beneath the water.

"Thanks," she said, dropping my hand once we stumbled ashore.

"No problem. It's not every day I get to save a lady who didn't need saving," I joked.

"I'm sure it's the thought that counts," she teased as we made our way up the embankment. Our steps squished as the leftover water seeped out over the tops of our shoes.

"Tell that to my ruined running shoes," I said, holding my muddy shoe up so she could see it.

"How about I give you a ride to make up for it? Although, I want the record to show I didn't ask you to go all stalker-hero and jump in after me," she teased between chattering lips.

"Fair enough, but next time you decide to do an adrenaline job, screaming less might be helpful."

"Point well taken," she agreed, pulling the passenger door open. "Here, you can have the towel since I have my sweatshirt," she added, tossing a folded-up towel at me.

"You should have taken off your wet shirt before you put that on," I pointed out, raising my eyebrows suggestively as she pulled the sweatshirt on over her wet T-shirt.

"I'm not that easy. You have to actually save me in order to get a boob shot," she quipped, climbing into the driver's seat.

Startled laughter bubbled up inside me. It had been a while since I'd been with someone so sassy. She was different than the refined, boring girls I normally dated. She was more open, with a sharper tongue that made me think about other things I'd like that tongue to do.

"Is that an invitation?" I asked, folding myself into the passenger seat.

"I'm not sure I have any more high-risk activities planned that will require your services."

"Maybe we can work out a side deal," I said, resting my arm on the back of the seat so my fingers were close to the nape of her neck without actually touching her. I bit back a smile when I saw a shudder of awareness ripple through her frame.

"What do you have in mind?" she asked, flipping the heat on as she whipped a U-turn in the middle of the road.

"Why don't you let me take you out to dinner and we can work out the particulars?" I answered, trailing my finger along the fine hair on her neck that had escaped the cute ponytail she wore on top of her head.

"There's not a whole lot of dining choices in Woodfalls unless you don't mind the diner. The better restaurants are in the next town, like twenty-five minutes away," she said, leaning back against my hand, which was now cupping her neck. I went instantly hard from the sigh of pleasure that escaped her mouth as I gently massaged her neck.

"Let me worry about dinner," I murmured, dipping my finger down the neckline of her shirt as she pulled her car into the parking lot of my motel. She switched off the car, but neither of us moved.

"This is crazy. We don't even know each other," she finally said hoarsely, cluing me in that she was as turned on as I was. Although, judging by her death grip on the steering wheel, she was trying to fight it.

"Go out with me and we'll get to know each other," I coaxed, sliding my hand farther down the back of her shirt. I watched as she gnawed on her bottom lip indecisively. I was more jealous of a set of teeth than I could have ever imagined possible. I wanted it to be my teeth that gently nipped on her lip. "Are you still worried I want to stick my trunk in your head?" I teased softly, trying to lighten the tension radiating off her.

"I'm not looking for a serious relationship," she mumbled.

"Let me get this straight. You're fine going out with me, but you just don't want me to get attached?" I asked, laughing at the irony of the situation. "Sweetheart, I have a strict rule about attachments, but that doesn't mean we can't have fun getting to know each other. Besides, I'll only be here a week or so."

"You won't fall in love with me?" she asked earnestly. Had the situation been different, I would have busted a gut at her question.

"I promise I won't fall in love with you," I said solemnly, since she seemed so serious. "How about if I promise that I plan to use you only for sex?" I joked.

"That would help," she said, nodding her head in total agreement.

"You know, this conversation is kind of messed up," I teased, trailing my hand a little farther down.

"I'm pretty sure everything we've done up to this point is messed up," she said, finally relaxing. "We might as well stay consistent."

"So, let me get this straight since I tend to look at things a bit analytically. It's okay if we date, but even better if I decide I want to ravish your body to my heart's content, and then walk away when I'm done?" I questioned.

"Exactly," she said, shivering slightly as my hand continued exploring.

"I'll pick you up at seven," I said, pulling her toward me. I settled my lips against hers for a moment, devouring the sigh of surprise that left her mouth. I pulled the lip that had been enticing me into my mouth and gave it a soft nip with my teeth. It tasted faintly like a combination of cherry lip gloss and minty mouthwash, but it was the heat that beckoned me. I could have made a feast of her lips and mouth. I wanted to explore every inch of them. After a moment, I forced myself to pull away and open my car door.

Her eyes looked at me questioningly as I stood outside her car. "Sorry, your bottom lip was driving me nuts. I had to see if it tasted as good as it looks," I explained.

"Well?" she asked, exasperated, as I started to close the door.

"Sweetheart, it tasted better than my wildest fantasies could have ever conjured up," I said, closing the door to her astonished face.

7. The Face Plant

ASHTON

I drove home in a fog after the earth-shattering kiss Nathan planted on me. "Earth-shattering" was so cliché, but this kiss was that and more. Never has a kiss affected me in so many different ways. The clumsy kisses I'd shared with a few boys in high school and college paled in comparison. It was the difference between ordering an aged steak at a five-star restaurant and the chopped meat patties they used to serve in the school cafeteria. His parting words, though, affected me the most. With just a few words, he made me feel desirable and cherished all at the same time.

Pulling in front of my cottage, I managed to clear the fog in my head long enough to go inside. Along the way, the cold air made its way through my wet clothes, chilling me to the bone and effectively putting out the rest of the fire he'd ignited inside me. My trembling fingers fumbled with my key until I was finally able to slide it into the lock. Closing the front door behind me, I began to strip down, leaving a trail of wet clothes behind me on my way to the bathroom. It took all the hot water the small water heater could muster to fight away the chills that had gripped me. Only when the water started to cool did I switch it off.

I stepped from the shower, quickly wrapping my body with a towel, and another turban-style around my head.

I was in the midst of pulling on skinny jeans and a cable-knit sweater when I heard my TV click on in the main room of the cottage.

"Want to hang out?" Tressa greeted me around a mouthful of gooey cheese pizza. "I figured we could watch a couple movies and gossip."

"God, Tressa. You scared the shit out of me," I said, even though the tantalizing smell of the pizza reminded me that I had skipped breakfast.

"Well, lock your door. You want some?" she asked, nodding toward the open pizza box on the table.

"Sure," I replied, grabbing a slice as I rounded up my wet clothes from the floor. Still munching along the way, I carried them to the utility room that had been built onto the back of the cottage. I shivered at the quickly dropping temperature outside and heaved the clothes into the basket so I could rush back inside.

"Man, it's crazy how quick the weather changes," I commented, heading back through the kitchen.

"Welcome to northern living, although it's not normally this cold in September. What I wouldn't give for warm weather all year around."

"Trust me. It's not as glamorous as it sounds. No seasons to speak of, and scorching summers take the fun out of warm-weather states. Did you bring chocolate too?" I asked, changing the subject as I sat down next to her.

"Chocolate fudge brownie ice cream," she answered, hitting the button on my Blu-ray player.

"Yum. What movies did you get in from Netflix?" I asked, grabbing another slice of pizza.

"This week it was comedies."

"Sounds good," I said, settling back against the cushions on my couch.

"So, are you going to tell me how your jump went, or am I supposed to brush up on my mind-reading skills?"

I took a moment to finish my second slice of pizza before answering her, unsure of how much information I wanted to divulge. "What makes you think I went through with it?"

"Uh, maybe because you left wet clothes strewn across your living room. Duh. I can't believe you were dumb enough to go by yourself."

I looked at her questionably.

"Brittni texted me about her strep to warn me. I'll probably get it next since the bitch took a swig of my beer the other night. So, spill it."

"I jumped off the bridge today," I said evasively.

"So help me, I will hit you upside the head with this remote if you don't answer my question," she threatened, holding up my remote like a weapon.

"Okay, psycho. I jumped, and it was scary, amazing, and exhilarating all wrapped up into one. I'd do it again if I hadn't frozen my ass off afterward. Well that, and if I hadn't been afraid the bridge was falling on top of me."

"What?"

"It would seem someone with a superhero complex was under the impression that I fell in and needed to be saved."

"OMG, please tell me it was Mr. Hot and Sexy who jumped in to save you," Tressa asked, bouncing on the couch with excitement.

"How did you know he was still in town?" I asked, surprised that was the natural conclusion she would reach.

"Hello. You do know this is Woodfalls, right? I could tell you who took a shit yesterday and who was constipated. The whole town is buzzing about the mysterious journalist who's decided to stick around in the boonies for a while. According to a very reliable source, he's super private and won't even let the maid service come in to clean his room. He has them drop off clean towels and sheets in the morning and leaves the dirty ones outside the door of his room," she said in an excited rush. "So, was he your knight in shining armor?"

"Wow, you're like Google; your knowledge knows no bounds," I joked, ignoring the way my heart rate had kicked into hyperdrive at the knowledge that he was sticking around for a while.

At my comment, she reached over and whacked me with the remote.

"Bitch, that hurt," I complained, rubbing my sore leg. "Fine," I said when she held up the remote again. "Yes, it was him. He nearly scared the shit out of me, jumping in after me like that. I was under the water when I heard a big-ass splash behind me. I was convinced that damn bridge was coming down."

"So, you're telling me this guy also has a hero complex? God, that's rich. Now I'm super bummed I didn't take him first the other night. I wouldn't mind a little mouth-to-mouth, if you catch my drift."

"I'd have to be in a mine shaft hundreds of miles beneath the earth not to catch your drift," I answered dryly. "It was sweet, but I'm not looking for some heavy relationship."

"Honey, neither am I, but that doesn't mean you can't have fun in the meantime. He's obviously panting after you like a dog. Use him for mind-blowing sex and move on," she said, grabbing a third slice of pizza.

"You sound like Fran. Aren't small-town girls supposed to have a higher sense of morals or something?"

"Honey, it's Sunday. Do you see me at any kind of church? Nope. My lack of morals was exposed many years ago. That and the fact that I may or may not have corrupted some of the boys when I was younger may have me on the 'we need to pray for her soul' list at all three churches in town. Seriously, though, they act like skinny-dipping in the baptism pool is frowned upon," she quipped, winking at me outrageously.

"Nuh-uh, please tell me you didn't," I asked, torn between laughter and horror. I wasn't a churchgoer, but I was sure that pretty much ranked up there with peeing in holy water or something like that.

"Only a couple of times."

"A couple of times?" I said, finally giving in to the urge of laughing.

"Okay, more like five times, but seriously, it was spread out at all three churches. So, really, it was closer to one and a half times at each church. No biggie," she said defensively.

"Well, that's one way to look at it, I guess. At least you were spreading the love—or boobies, more accurately," I teased, pointedly eyeing her large chest, which never seemed to want to stay confined beneath the material of her shirts.

"Truth. These babies deserve to be shared," she answered, cupping her breasts for emphasis.

"Does that mean you've decided to break it off with Jackson again?" I asked, naming her on-again, off-again boyfriend who drove me more than a little batty.

"Yeah," she said, looking guilty. "I just couldn't take it anymore. His dumb-ass mom is forever feeding his head with stories about how a good girl should act. She has him convinced he's going to go to hell for sticking it in me before marriage. She's always telling him we're too young for sex and not mature enough to handle it. I swear I feel like I'm back in high school rather than my senior year of college. I like him and all, but he seriously needs to figure out the kind of man he wants to be. Either he's a man who has his own mind, or he's a momma's boy. Regardless, I'm sick of holding his hands through his guilt. He gets all excited during the whole act, but after it's over, he acts like he's run over a dog or something."

"His mom would shit if she knew how many teens were sexually active at my old high school, and it was even worse at college. She should be happy you two are at least adults. Are you going to drop him for good this time?"

"I think so. There's a guy in my Psych Two class who's been asking me out since the semester started."

"Good for you," I said, not admitting that I'd always questioned her and Jackson's relationship. I'd seen his wishy-washy attitude about things firsthand. Plus, he was a total douche about letting Tressa do certain things, like attend parties closer to her college. He had once commented that she was lucky he allowed her to make the forty-five-minute commute to her campus each day. I had to fight the urge not to punch him in the throat for that one.

"You think so?" she asked, sounding insecure for the first time since we'd become friends.

"Absolutely. You totally deserve someone who's not constantly belittling you when he's not trying to sex you up."

"It feels scary," she admitted. "We've been on a break before, but we've never dated other people, and we've been together practically since we were freshmen in high school."

I nodded my head, already knowing everything she was saying. As far as I was concerned, seven years of bullshit was seven years too many. "I think you're making the right decision. You deserve way more than that momma's boy is willing to give you," I reassured her. "When are you going out with the guy from your class?"

"His name is Greg, and next Friday. We're going to go listen to some new band everyone's been raving about. They're supposed to be a-fucking-mazing. You and Britt should come check them out."

"Right, because having your two best friends tag along with you on your first date isn't a buzzkill. Besides, Brittni leaves in the morning for the internship training thing."

"Don't be a smart-ass. I meant you guys should go and check it out too. Maybe we could go check them out tonight before Britt heads out."

"Can't tonight," I said around a mouthful of pizza.

"Why not?"

"I kind of told Nathan I'd go out with him tonight."

"Are you fucking with me? You've known this whole time I've been here that you're going out with the make-me-wet stranger and you're just now mentioning it?" she yelled, whacking me with the remote again.

"So help me God, if you hit me with that remote again, you'll find it shoved somewhere you don't want it."

"Oh, you flirt. Now, stop coming on to me and spill it," Tressa demanded, muting the TV as if my news required absolute silence to be revealed.

"It's really no biggie. I think Nathan and I have tentatively agreed to date with a possibility of it turning into an affair with no attachments," I squawked out. Our deal suddenly seemed utterly ridiculous when steam and heat weren't clouding my judgment.

"Holy shit, you slut," she joked as I glared at her. "Kidding."

"I must be insane, right?" I moaned, covering my face with my hands.

"If that's insanity, break me off a piece. I'll take a no-strings kind of arrangement with him any day. So, where's he taking you?"

"I'm not sure," I admitted, rising from the sofa so I could calm my nerves with a mind-numbing amount of ice cream. "He said he'd take care of it when I pointed out Woodfalls isn't really known for its restaurant choices," I added, grabbing two bowls from the cabinet.

"Hey, that's not true. Now that they finally finished the McDonald's by the high school, we're completely chic," she mocked.

"Right you are. There's absolutely nothing wrong with gazing into each other's eyes over a cheeseburger and fries."

"Honey, I'm sure he won't be gazing into your eyes," she teased, looking at my chest.

"Stop being a perv. Besides, my boobs are nowhere near as big as yours," I answered, taking a big bite of ice cream so I wouldn't have to say anything else. A moment later, I yelped in pain as the ice cream hit my head in the worst case of brain freeze ever.

"Sheesh, dip, didn't anyone ever teach you to take smaller bites?" Tressa asked, handing over her glass of water. "I feel like I'm babysitting Mackenzie and Matthew," she teased, referring to her niece and nephew, two-year-old twins.

I would have glared at her, but my head wasn't quite over the stabbing sensation I was currently suffering from. After several moments, I was finally able to resume eating my ice cream in the smaller increments that Tressa took it upon herself to remind me to take. We spent the rest of the afternoon laughing our way through the comedies she had brought over. I pushed thoughts of Nathan to the far recesses of my brain, but every once in a while they would pop in just to frazzle me throughout the afternoon. By the time Tressa gathered her stuff to leave, I gave up all pretenses of normalcy.

"You'll be fine," she said, giving me a hard hug in typical Tressa fashion.

"I'm not worried," I blatantly lied through a fake smile.

"Right. Your face is always a delicate shade of green," she said, laughing. "You'll be fine," she repeated. "Just enjoy the ride," she added, wagging her eyebrows at me suggestively. "And I mean that in every sense of the word."

"You're not helping," I griped, shooing her out the front door.

"I expect tons of text messages and a call first thing in the morning," she yelled through my front door as I sagged against it. I was a mess. I seriously needed to get my shit together before Nathan saw through my adolescent hang-ups.

The next hour passed in a frenzied whirlwind of activity as I exhibited behaviors of someone who didn't have their shit together at all. I had decided to keep my attire casual and wear the cable-knit sweater and jeans I already had on.

Halfway through brushing my hair, I had a sudden panic attack that my legs weren't freshly shaved. Dropping my jeans to my ankles, I rubbed my hand down my legs, grimacing at the short stubble that covered them. I glanced at the clock on my nightstand. Six forty-five; shit, maybe I had enough time to quickly run a razor over them.

With my jeans still around my ankles, I hobbled toward the bathroom, which wasn't the best idea with my brain so frazzled. I took a face-first header into the wooden floors of my room, and it knocked the breath right out of me. Gasping, I took stock of any possible injuries while I ignored the dust bunnies under my bed, which I now had a bird's-eye view of. Of course, it would be at that moment that Nathan decided to knock on my front door.

I jumped to my feet, forgetting once again that my jeans were still around my ankles.

"Mother of all fuck," I grumbled as I found myself flat on my stomach for the second time with a loud crash. My lungs had just forgiven me for my last fall, and now they seized up again, making me gasp for breath like a drowning victim. Halfway between berating myself for my complete dipshitted-ness and wishing my floor were at least carpeted in a situation like this, I heard my front door open.

"Ashton, are you okay?" Nathan's worried voice called out.

I was in hell. For the briefest of moments, I actually contemplated trying to slide under my bed to hide. Tressa was right. I really needed to start locking my door.

"I'm fine," I answered, using the little bit of breath I had managed to recoup. I frantically tried to shimmy my jeans up over my legs, although my prone position wasn't helping much.

"I thought someone was attacking you," the last voice I wanted to hear at the moment said from my bedroom doorway.

I was wrong before. *This* was hell. "That someone would be my jeans." My answer came out muddled thanks to my predicament as heat filled my cheeks.

"Are you okay?" he asked, obviously concerned to see my panty-covered ass sticking up while I tried in vain to hide my face in the wood flooring.

"By okay, if you mean, 'Would I like to die at the moment?' that would be a resounding yes." My voice came out muffled due to the wood flooring against my face.

"Would you like my help?" he asked. Now that he knew I hadn't suffered a stroke or cracked my head wide open, he was completely amused.

"No, I think I can handle this," I said sarcastically, flipping over onto my back so I could hike up my jeans. It was only after I was in the middle of doing so that I realized my sweater had hiked up to my neck, exposing my bra-covered chest.

"I kind of thought we would work up to this, but hey, I'm all in," he joked, leaning against the doorjamb.

"Seriously, God must hate me," I mumbled, abandoning my jeans so I could pull down my sweater. "I'll be out in a minute," I said, trying to salvage the smallest bit of dignity I had left.

"Are you sure? I have no problem assisting you," he said, winking at me.

"Out," I demanded, trying to ignore the heat that flowed through me from his wink. It was unfair that even in my mortification, his wink had the power to seduce me.

He chuckled, pulling my bedroom door closed behind him and leaving me alone in my misery.

8. *Appetizer, Anyone?*

NATHAN

I pulled into Ashton's driveway ten minutes early and debated waiting in the car for a few minutes. As a rule, I never showed up early for a date. Women appreciated punctuality but loathed being surprised with an early arrival. As with everything concerning Ashton, all my rules were a wash. I wanted to see her, and I didn't want to wait.

I tried to at least discipline myself to walk to the front door like I had some kind of control. I knocked, expecting her to answer, but was surprised when I heard a dull thump from within the cottage like something had fallen or had been knocked down. Going by instinct, I reached out and tried the doorknob. Finding it unlocked, I pushed the door open and stepped inside. Adrenaline raced through me as I heard struggling coming from the other room. Calling out to Ashton was only a formality since there was no way in hell I was waiting around to see if someone was attacking her or something to that effect. Her muffled response only fueled my fire as I prepared to kick someone's ass. Little did I know what I would find instead.

What was perhaps the finest panty-covered ass I had ever seen greeted me. Seeing that Ashton wasn't being attacked, I allowed myself to enjoy the show. My offer of assistance made her creamy skin take on an enticing shade of pink that begged to be touched with my hands and lips.

By the time she had regained her composure long enough to kick me out, I was fully aroused and fighting the temptation to scoop her up in my arms and tumble down on the bed that was practically calling my name.

Fifteen minutes later, Ashton emerged from her room with all her clothes in their rightful places. "Not one word," she threatened as I appraised her appearance.

I couldn't help throwing my head back and laughing at her feisty tone. I was used to dating women who were dull in their refined ways. Very rarely did they lose their cool, and they never said anything without weighing their words carefully first. Somewhere along the way, I had convinced myself that was what I wanted. Being with Ashton's quick tongue gave me a glimpse of what I had been missing. In the last forty-eight hours, she had made me laugh more than I had with all the women I had been with combined.

"I wouldn't dream of saying anything," I answered, rising from the couch.

I smiled as she took a visibly relieved breath.

"Ready to go?" I asked.

"Yes," she answered, obviously ready to leave behind the scene of the crime.

Chuckling at the evident relief in her voice, I innocently placed my hand on the small of her back. The warmth of her skin beneath her sweater made me feel nothing close to gentlemanly as I guided her toward the door. Looking her up and down from behind, I wondered if her smooth skin would feel as soft against my lips as it had looked a few minutes prior.

No longer able to resist, I turned her body with my hand until she was facing me.

She looked up at me with hooded eyes, and I could tell my touch was affecting her much in the same manner it was me. Without pause, I crushed my lips to hers. Unlike the kiss earlier that day, there was nothing playful about this one. I needed her to know just how badly I wanted her. I dragged her into my arms until her body was flush against mine, devouring her sigh of surprise as she felt my arousal. Our tongues merged together in a tantalizing dance. Each stroke made the fire inside me burn hotter, consuming me. In a more rational part of my brain, I worried I was hurting her as I crushed her even tighter in my arms, but when I tried to pull back, her hands reached up to my head, pulling me closer. This time it was me who groaned in surprise as she took control of the kiss. She rubbed her body seductively against mine, grinding her hips against the bulge that wanted to burst out of my jeans. I placed my hands firmly around her waist and backed her up against the door so she could feel exactly what she was doing to me. She moaned with pleasure and hiked up a leg around me, keeping me pinned against her. With one hand, I held her leg up and rolled my hips, smiling with satisfaction as she panted against my lips with need. She was close to the point of no return and I could sense by her erratic movements that the sensation was new to her. The need to bury myself in her was overpowering, but I ignored my own needs as I rocked against her again. She whimpered against my lips. Breaking the kiss, I trailed my lips over her cheek and past her neck until they were on her ear. Gripping her ass in my free hand, I pulled her as close to me as our clothed state would allow.

"Let it come," I murmured in her ear, rocking against her one last time. The shudders radiated throughout her body as her release took over.

"Oh, God," she sighed once the quaking in her body was under control. "I'm pretty sure I should be mortified at what just happened, but oh, God," she repeated, dropping her head to my chest as her soft body sagged against mine.

"That may be the single most erotic moment of my life," I said, dropping a kiss on the back of her exposed neck.

"How is that possible? You didn't . . . uh," she stammered as embarrassment finally reared its head. "We could-d-d go to m-m-my room," she offered, stumbling over her words.

"It was erotic because you make the most amazing noises

when you enjoy something. As enticing as your bedroom sounds, I think I'll allow the intensity of the main course to build since the appetizer was so delectable," I breathed into her ear before dropping a hard kiss on her lips. "Now, let's go eat before I take you up on your offer."

9. *A First Date from Hell*

ASHTON

My legs were still shaking as Nathan helped me into his Range Rover. I was embarrassed at my wanton behavior, but I couldn't help thinking how good his body had felt against mine. His lips heated me from the inside out while his movements had done things my body had never felt before. I'd seen plenty of movies and heard girls talking about it over the years, but I'd been pretty convinced they overglorified what an orgasm felt like. I mean, really, how could it be so fantastic when girls often used the same word to describe a delicious bite of food or chocolate? Now I knew. What I had just experienced went beyond food or chocolate. Nothing compared to it.

"So, what are you thinking?" Nathan teased, climbing into the driver's seat.

I flushed, making it clear where my thoughts had just been. I glanced out the window, willing my blush to disappear.

"Sweetheart, there's nothing to be embarrassed about," Nathan said, reaching over to pat my knee before resting his hand there.

The heat of his palm burned through my pants, making me shift slightly as desire slowly crept in again. I was shocked that I wanted him again so quickly.

"It's just new to me," I admitted, biting my lip.

"Are you a virgin?" he asked frankly as his hand tightened slightly on my knee.

"No," I answered, feeling myself blush all over again. "Would it matter?" I asked, curious as to what he was thinking.

"Yes, no—I don't know. If you were, it would change things," he admitted.

"How so?" I asked, more than a little curious about what that had to do with anything.

"It probably wouldn't sit well if I took your virginity in this 'no-attachments' arrangement we have going on."

"So, why were you unsure a minute ago? You first said yes, but then changed to no."

"That was the greedy bastard in me talking. I'd like nothing more than to be the only person who has had these legs wrapped around him," he answered, stroking my leg with his hand for emphasis.

"Oh," I said, licking my suddenly dry lips at his words. It was overwhelming how a few simple words could leave me squirming with anticipation.

"You really need to not do that while I'm driving," he chastised.

"Do what?"

"Gnaw on your lip. You know damn well what you're doing," he said, tightening his hand on my leg.

The power I seemed to hold over him right now made me smile, but I settled back in my seat as he merged onto the highway. We rode in silence for several minutes as the desire that burned between us simmered down to a low sizzle.

"So, where are you from, Ashton?" he asked, breaking the silence.

I weighed my answer carefully before speaking. I was unsure how much of my past I was willing to divulge. "Florida," I finally answered, ignoring the knot of tension in my stomach.

"Really? Me too. Whereabouts?" he asked conversationally.

The interior of the vehicle felt like it was closing in around me. I instantly regretted my honesty. I should have made up another state. "Um, near Palm Coast," I lied, naming a city miles away from my true hometown. "What about you?" I asked, silently praying he didn't say Palm Coast too.

"Over near Tampa," he answered as I let out a pent-up breath.

"That's a nice area," I answered, breathing easier.

"Like every city, it has its good and bad areas. I've lived in both."

I nodded my head like I could relate, when in reality I couldn't. My family had never wanted for anything. My grandfather made a name for himself in computer software before anyone realized how much computers would affect their lives. My father followed in his footsteps by designing computer programs before he even graduated from high school. Money was never an issue for me. I had gone to the best schools, hung out with the wealthiest of kids, and went to the college of my choice. My life had been steeped in privilege. Of course, no amount of money can protect you from the harsh cards life can deal you.

"Do your parents still live there?" I finally asked when the silence between us stretched.

He shook his head. "No, my mom died a while back," he answered.

"I'm sorry," I said, resting my hand on top of his. "Mine died when I was ten," I added before I could stop myself.

"Ten? That's rough."

"Yeah, it was a tough time for me. She was so filled with life that it was almost like someone had snuffed out the sun when she died."

"How did she die, if you don't mind me asking?" he asked.

"Ovarian cancer. She was bad about going to doctors when she felt crummy. By the time they discovered it, it was too late. My dad took her to the hospital when she finally confessed something was wrong. She never came home," I said, trying to forget how my father had looked the night he had come home after she died. He'd looked like he'd been hit by a train. The light in his eyes went out that night and didn't return until many years later.

"Shit. I'm sorry," he said, flipping his hand over so he could lace his fingers through mine.

"It's life," I said, shrugging like it didn't matter, even though her death had shaped the person I was. I often wondered if my life would have turned out differently if she were still alive.

"It sucks, plain and simple," he said, seeing through my lie.

"What about your dad?" I asked, changing the subject. I was surprised when his hand spasmed in mine before abruptly releasing it. He gripped the steering wheel hard enough to make his knuckles turn white and his expression became unreadable. I was taken aback by the tension that radiated off him.

"I'm not sure. I haven't spoken to the son of a bitch since he left my mom and me practically homeless so he could screw his secretary full-time," he clipped out. Silence filled the vehicle. I wondered indecisively if I should comment or change the subject.

"Fuck, whose idea was it to talk about family?" he asked wryly as some of the tension finally began to leave him.

"I think that honor falls on you," I said, smiling weakly at him.

"Well, that was a shitty idea. Let's talk about something more interesting."

"Sounds like a plan," I agreed. "Did you always want to be a journalist?" I asked, taking charge of the conversation.

"Not really, I kind of fell into it. When I was younger, I wanted to be a cop. You know, catch the bad guys and save the day. When I was in high school, I discovered I was pretty good at writing. For a while, I entertained the idea of becoming an investigative journalist, but it never panned out. How about you?"

"You mean, did I always dream about working in some general store in the middle of nowhere?" I joked. "I actually wanted to be a children's psychologist in a hospital," I answered truthfully, ignoring the knots that had returned full force in my stomach.

"What changed?" he asked, taking his eyes off the road long enough to peer at me.

"Life," I answered truthfully. "Sometimes life throws you a curveball and either you duck to avoid it, or you swing at it with all your might."

"Which option did you take?"

"Neither. I chose option three, which was to walk away."

"It's never too late to go back and swing," he said, pulling into the parking lot of a quaint-looking Italian restaurant.

"I don't want to swing," I said, trying to keep my voice light.

"So, you plan on working at Fran's until you die?" he asked, sounding irritated.

"That's not really any of your business, is it, since this is supposed to be a *no-attachments* relationship?" I snapped.

"Hell, you're right. It's none of my business," he said, raking his fingers through his hair.

"Maybe a no-attachments relationship isn't possible. We can't seem to make it an hour without delving into no-man's-land," I said, staring out my window, waiting for him to start the vehicle back up and take me home. We'd have to chalk up the whole charade as a failure.

I jumped when Nathan opened his door and abruptly left the vehicle. He came around the Range Rover to my side. Opening the door, he stepped closer, unlatched my seat belt, and pivoted my legs around in the seat so they were straddling him where he stood. "We can figure this out," he said.

"Are you sure?" I whispered as his lips lowered to mine.

"I'm positive," he said, pulling my bottom lip gently into his mouth before releasing it. "It's like learning to ride a bike. Sure, we're going to fall over a couple times, but the important thing is that we keep getting back on," he added, settling his lips firmly on mine. "You willing to give it a ride?" he asked, pulling back.

"As long as you don't fall in love with riding that bike," I emphasized.

"Darling, I'm not going to lie. I'm going to enjoy riding that bike probably more than any other bike I've ever ridden, but I won't fall in love with it," he reassured me, hiking my leg up around his waist. "The question is: Will you fall in love with the bike ride?"

"It's not possible for me to fall in love with any bike ride," I replied earnestly. "Not anymore, anyway," I added, working to keep the pain the words caused out of my voice.

His eyes narrowed slightly and he looked like he wanted to say something, but instead, he reached out to help me climb from the vehicle. "Let's eat," was all he said.

"How'd you find this place?" I asked as he held open the door of the restaurant for me.

"I asked Fran. I figured she wouldn't steer me wrong. Have you been here before?"

"No, I really haven't ventured out of Woodfalls much since I moved there. I guess small-town life has not caught up to me. Although, now that I'm here, it smells delicious," I answered as the scents of herbs and spices enticed my nose.

"So, why Woodfalls?" he asked once we were seated.

"I wanted something that was completely different than Florida. Changing seasons, snow and ice skating, things like that, so I drove until I figured I was far enough north to get all of those. We never really went on vacation again after my mom died, so if I ever saw snow, I really don't remember it."

"No ski vacations while you were in college?" he inquired, handing me a bread stick from the basket the waitress had placed on our table.

"What makes you think I went to college?" I asked.

"Did you?" he countered.

"Well, yeah, but it's presumptuous to think I automatically went. Plenty of people never go to college."

"Why do you get so prickly when I ask about your past?" he asked.

I debated his question for a moment before answering. "I'm just not crazy talking about it. It's not a time of my life I like to talk about," I said, letting him know he was entering no-man's-land again.

"Fair enough," he said, holding his hands up in surrender. "What's your favorite color?" he asked, switching gears.

"It depends on my mood. What about you?" I asked, grateful he'd let the subject drop without making a big deal of it.

"I would have to say the same. Although, I have found recently I'm quite fond of pink," he said, leaning over the small round table to brush his thumb over my bottom lip to emphasize his point. "I'm sure different shades of pink will be my favorite for a while," he added, dropping his eyes to my chest to make his point clear.

"Do come-ons like that always work for you?" I asked, working not to blush at his innuendo.

"You tell me," he said, sitting back in his seat with a small smile.

"We'll see," I answered, laughing breathlessly.

"Ooh, good answer. Okay, dogs or cats?" he asked, switching gears again.

"I'm not really sure. I never had any pets growing up. Probably a cat, though. I always had this dream that my dad would surprise me with a kitten or something for my birthday," I said, surprised at the wistful tone in my voice. "How about you?"

"I have a cat that gets taken care of by my neighbor while I'm away on my extended trips. He's a cool cat, but he holds a slight grudge when I leave him. I know not to arrive at my condo without treats and a toy," he answered in a warm voice that melted me inside. Who knew a man who loved cats would come across so hot?

"A toy?" I asked, intrigued. "Do cats play with things other than strings or a paper ball?"

"He's not into the typical cat toys. He has a particular lid fetish."

"Lid fetish?" I asked, raising my eyebrows.

"Like from hair spray bottles," he explained.

I looked at him blankly, not quite sure that I knew what he was talking about, although he looked quite adorable trying to explain it.

"You know, the small lids that cover the spray nozzles," he said, holding his fingers about an inch apart for emphasis. Seeing my amusement, he plunged on.

"Anyway, he likes it when you throw one across the ceramic floor. He'll run after it and bring it back like a dog. So whenever I'm gone, I make a point of getting several of the lids for him."

"Do you really go through that much hair spray?"

"Well, no. I guess you could say I save other consumers the hassle of removing the lids off their bottles," he said sheepishly while I laughed.

"So, you mean to tell me your cat has turned you into a lid thief?"

"Well, when you put it that way, I guess so. Did I mention he was a cool cat?"

"He sounds like it," I said sincerely. The idea of Nathan strolling down the beauty aisle of a store, leaving behind a row of lidless hair spray bottles, cracked me up. "Your neighbor doesn't mind watching him?" I asked.

"Nah, she claims it's no problem at all."

"How old would this neighbor happen to be?"

"I don't know, early twenties," he answered as the waitress approached to take our orders.

"I bet she doesn't mind," I said dryly once the waitress had taken our orders. I tried to convince myself I didn't feel jealous. What did it matter to me if his neighbor had the hots for him?

"Is that a note of jealousy I hear?" he teased.

"Of course not. As long as she's not on the bike while I'm on it, I have no complaints," I sniped.

"Now that is something I would like to see," he said eagerly.

"I bet you would," I said, tossing a small piece of bread at him.

"As enticing at it sounds to have both of you on the bike with me, I'm perfectly content to just ride it with you," he added in a husky voice that made me uncross my legs in anticipation. "I foresee a long bike ride in our future," he added, barely looking up when the waitress dropped our salads off at the table. I felt his leg nudge mine under the small table before rubbing seductively against me.

"Really?" I asked, working to keep my breathing even. "You seem awfully confident about your bike-riding skills." I flirted back, shocking myself at my innuendo.

"Darling, I can guarantee you've never had a bike ride like the one I'm going to take you on. It'll make what happened in your living room earlier seem like a tricycle ride," he murmured, rubbing his thumb across the pulse point on my wrist.

I was embarrassed over the reminder, but his words also

brought back the mental picture of our bodies tangled together, and what he had done to me.

As if he sensed my thoughts, his own eyes darkened with desire. Withdrawing my hand from his, I focused on eating my salad so I could get my raging hormones under control. My efforts were futile. My appetite was nonexistent in light of what we could be doing. By keeping my eyes down and focusing on my salad, I felt some semblance of normalcy. I figured Nathan was having a similar issue with focusing when I heard him clear his throat twice in quick succession. It was only when he did it a third time that I finally looked up. I was shocked to see that his face looked slightly distorted. His lips seemed swollen like someone had blown them up slightly. His cheeks were puffed out like he was a squirrel storing nuts for the winter. He tried to clear his throat again, but it came out more of a gurgle.

Finally realizing what was happening, I jumped to my feet. "Are you allergic to nuts?" I asked, thinking about the salad we had just been consuming.

He tried to talk again, to no avail.

"What's going on?" the waitress asked, placing our plates on the table as she eyed Nathan's rapidly swelling face in horror.

"Are there nuts in the salad?" I demanded.

"Crushed cashews," she said weakly as I helped Nathan to his feet.

"A warning label would have been nice," I snapped. "How far to the nearest hospital?"

"Less than five minutes," one of the other patrons said,

joining us. "You can follow me," she said, grabbing her purse and her young daughter.

"Thank you," I said, helping Nathan out of the restaurant.

"No problem. My sister is allergic to nuts too. Normally she carries an EpiPen wherever she goes," she said, looking at me questioningly.

"Do you have an EpiPen in your car?" I asked Nathan, who was struggling to drag air through his windpipe. He shook his head no.

"Well, that's not very smart," I snapped, depositing him in the passenger seat. By the time I climbed behind the wheel, the lady from the restaurant was already waiting for me in her vehicle by the exit. Once I put the vehicle into gear, she tore out of the parking lot with me right behind her.

I glanced over at Nathan while I drove, not liking the purplish tint his face had taken. Gripping the steering wheel hard, I continued to berate him in my panic-filled state. I knew it wasn't the best time to be ridiculing him, but my frustration at the situation had me rambling on. Thankfully, the traffic lights were on our side as we sped down the road. Finally, I could see the hospital in the distance. The traffic light just before the hospital turned yellow and we were still more than a hundred yards back, but both of us stepped on the accelerator and ran the red light before screeching into the hospital ambulance bay.

"Hey, you can't park here," a nurse said as I threw open my door.

"My friend is having an allergic reaction," I hurled at her as I raced around the vehicle to open his door.

The nurse took one look at Nathan slumped over in the passenger seat before hollering out instructions to the other staff as the double doors to the ER slid open. The next few minutes passed in a blur as medical staff descended on Nathan's car. Before I knew it, they were wheeling him into the ER on a gurney. I stood in the now-empty ambulance bay, completely at a loss for what I should be doing. A kind security guard took pity on me and pointed me in the direction of where I could park. I got back behind the wheel and drove the vehicle to the proper location. Moving in a haze, I tried to focus on anything but my aversion to hospitals as I made my way to the admittance desk.

"Can I help you?" the receptionist asked without looking up.

"Um, yeah, I'm looking for my friend," I said, figuring *bike-riding partner* wouldn't be much of an explanation.

"Name," she asked, looking bored.

"Nathan," I said, tapping my foot impatiently.

"I don't see a patient by that name. Are you sure this is the right hospital?" she asked, resuming her typing.

"Considering the fact that I drove him here five minutes ago and watched members of your staff wheel him through those double doors, I would say yeah, I'm sure I have the right hospital," I answered sarcastically.

"What is his injury?" she asked, not responding in the slightest to my sarcasm.

"Allergic reaction," I said, working to keep my voice even while I fought the urge to grab her Snoopy-covered hospital scrubs and shake the hell out of her.

"Curtain five," she said, pointing to the other side of the room, which was partitioned by curtains hanging from the ceiling.

"Thanks," I muttered, hurrying off.

Sweeping into the curtained-off area, I was unprepared for the sight that greeted me.

An elderly doctor was intently listening to Nathan's lungs with a stethoscope, but it was the actual sight of a shirtless Nathan that stopped me in my tracks.

10. *A Night in the Hospital*

NATHAN

I would have been amused by Ashton's expression when she entered my not-so-private room if not for the fact that I felt like a complete bonehead. A bonehead with lips the size of watermelon slices and cheeks that felt numb from the rapid swelling they had endured. I felt the pain was justified for being a complete ass. First, by not checking my salad more thoroughly, and second, for forgetting to throw a spare EpiPen in the glove compartment.

"Your lungs sound clear, which is a good sign. Don't worry about the swelling. It will dissipate soon. You will have to spend the night with us so we can pump fluids into you," the doctor said, pointing to my IV.

"Do you really think that's necessary?" I rasped out.

"It's not even debatable," he said on his way out. "A nurse

should be in here shortly so we can take you to your room," he threw over his shoulder.

"How are you doing?" Ashton asked, approaching hesitantly.

"Truth or macho guy answer?" I asked.

"Why don't we go with the truth since *truthfully* you look like shit," she said, sliding the only chair in the small cubicle toward my bed.

"Don't try to spare my feelings," I tried to joke through a harsh cough.

"Wouldn't dream of it, but seriously, if you didn't want to go on a bike ride, all you had to do was just say so," she teased, lacing her fingers through mine.

"Well, I did promise it would be a ride you wouldn't easily forget," I replied ruefully.

"Well, you pulled that off."

"Told you," I said, bringing her hand up to my lips so I could place a kiss on her knuckles. "You don't need to wait around here. You can take my car home and I can catch a cab in the morning when they release me."

"Don't be silly. I have nowhere to go. I'll keep you company until they move you to a room, and I'll be here in the morning to pick you up. Don't even think of arguing," she said before I could speak again.

"I wouldn't dream of it," I said, holding up my hands in surrender.

"So, are there any other allergies I need to be aware of?" she asked, raising her eyebrow at me.

"Don't think so. Truthfully, I don't give the cashew one much thought. It's not like it's a common ingredient in anything. It was just rotten luck that the restaurant decided to use cashews for a topping. I usually carry a spare EpiPen, but I haven't had a reaction in years. You know, I could blame you," I teased.

"Me?" she asked, sounding shocked by my accusation.

"Hell, yeah. If you hadn't been seducing me in the middle of the restaurant, I would have paid more attention to what I was putting in my mouth."

"Surely someone of your experience would know what to put in your mouth," she said saucily.

Her not-so-subtle innuendo rekindled my arousal from earlier. I had to adjust the blanket across my lap to hide the evidence. "Honey, normally it's not a problem," I said, only to choke slightly on my vocal cords, which still weren't cooperating.

She laughed while I stuttered over a cough. "I think you'll have to save your flirting for another day, hot stuff," she said, gently pushing my shoulders until I was lying back against the hospital bed, which was slightly inclined. Still coughing, I nodded in defeat. Tonight, I was barely any talk with definitely no action. I would have been highly disappointed at the way the night had gone if I didn't have the mental picture of the appetizer at her house to fall back on.

Ashton stayed with me during the few hours it took to get me into a room. We continued to skirt away from the tougher subjects and instead talked about the things we loved. It didn't surprise me in the slightest that Ashton was bright and intuitive on most subjects. Her insights into pop culture were a nice change from the boring conversations I was used to. It was refreshing to talk about our taste in music, books, and movies. As luck would have it, though, the medicine they were pumping through me began to take effect and my eyelids grew heavy. I only meant to close them for a second, but it was like they'd been superglued down. I felt Ashton pulling the covers over me and I would have thanked her, but the meds and a sudden headache pulled me under. I thought I felt her hand graze the planes of my chest, then trickle down my stomach. Maybe it was just the meds, or I could have been dreaming, but either way, I liked it. One thing was clear: Ashton was nothing like I expected. How was I going to get her out of my system when everything about her seemed to pull me in?

11. *Anticipating the Deed*

ASHTON

Despite the fact that he had fallen asleep, I stayed with Nathan as promised until they moved him to his room. Only once he was out did I allow myself to dwell on how scared I had been, thinking he was going to die. We'd only been together for a couple of days and really knew nothing about each other, yet I was worrying about him like we had been lovers for a lifetime. It was insanity to feel anything other than lust for someone I hardly knew, but everything about him enticed me, tricking me into believing in what-ifs. We weren't supposed to have any feelings or strings attached, but here I was. I knew without a shadow of a doubt I was setting myself up. The wisest thing I could do would be to catch a cab and never look back. No harm, no foul. Foolishly, I did neither.

The drive back to my cottage passed quickly as I attempted

to sort through and categorize my feelings. By the time I returned home, I realized my mixed-up emotions were an accumulation of stress and anxiety from his allergic reaction. Sure, I liked him, but he was still just an item on my list. I had to stick to our deal, and as long as he could keep his word, we could have our fun and then go our separate ways.

The chirping of a new text on my phone woke me the next morning.

I smiled when I read the text message from Tressa.

Give me all the deets Ho.

Can't. It would take forever to type all the deets.

OMG you dirty Ho. Too many deets? I think I need to take a cold shower.

Don't be a perv, I typed, laughing.

Takes one to know one. Now dish the juicy deets.

Can't I have to run an errand. I'll call you later after I get off work.

I was anxious to go, and hurried off to the bathroom to get ready. I wanted to convince myself that my nervous energy was just because I had to hurry and pick him up and get back in time for work, but the truth was I wanted to see him again. The magnetic pull we seemed to have taunted me with its insistence. Thoughts of the kiss we had shared the night before flashed through my head as I showered. How good it felt to have his hands on me with his body flush against mine. The desire flowing through me was overwhelming as I allowed my fantasy to continue. My hands followed the path of the warm water cascading down the curves of my body. I felt myself swaying as I imagined Nathan's tongue on my skin. "Okay, I don't have time for this," I said aloud, snapping myself back to reality. I switched the water to the coldest setting to clear my head and finished my shower. The bathroom felt chilly as I wrapped the towel around me and hurried to my room to dress.

Ten minutes later, I was backing Nathan's SUV out of my driveway, headed for the hospital. While I sat at a traffic light about five miles from the hospital, curiosity got the better of me, and I couldn't help snooping around his vehicle. The middle console held nothing but loose change and a container of orange Tic Tacs, which I found cute. The light changed before I could further my search. Only when I was parked in the visitor lot at the hospital was I able to continue snooping. I was a bit disappointed when the glove compartment yielded nothing but an insurance card, registration, and a vehicle owner's manual. I don't know what I was hoping to find. Maybe a picture or something that would give me insight into his life.

I began to feel guilty about looking through his stuff, especially considering I had set the rules for our relationship.

Deciding to give it a rest, I climbed from the vehicle and headed toward the entrance of the hospital. Nathan's room was up on the third floor. When I reached his room, I paused outside his door when I heard him talking.

"It was a dead end," I heard him say. I realized the silence that followed his comment meant he was on the phone. Feeling intrusive, I started to back away when his next comment stopped me in his tracks.

"It could take several weeks. I'll backtrack to see if I can catch what I missed."

Several more moments of silence followed before he harshly responded again. "You can certainly do that. I don't see them yielding any different results, but it's your money."

More silence.

"I think that's a wise decision. I'll call you in a few weeks when I have something solid to report," Nathan said.

Pushing open his door, I was surprised to find him already dressed and sitting at the foot of his bed. His expression was sullen until he spotted me in the doorway. I felt bad that his boss was giving him a hard time.

"Your boss being a douche?" I asked, indicating the phone in his hand.

Nathan eyed me warily for a moment before sighing heavily. "He's not pleased with the story I'm currently working on," he said, studying me intently.

"Does that mean you're leaving?" I asked, acting like it didn't matter either way.

He smiled at me, looking relieved. "Not on your life, sweetheart. He can suffer it out," he added with sudden steel in his voice.

"Will he fire you?" I asked.

"If he does, there are other jobs. I'm not worried," he said, sliding an arm around me and guiding me out of the room.

"Don't you need to wait to be discharged?"

"Already done. I could have gone home last night. I woke up around two feeling completely normal. Of course, the doctor kept me waiting until he made his rounds this morning."

"Poor baby," I teased, pushing the down button for the elevator.

"Damn straight," he growled, pulling me even closer once we stepped into the empty elevator. "I was left for hours with only thoughts of you to keep me entertained since the TV in my room was broken."

"Is that a bad thing?" I asked as he turned me to face him.

"Only in the aspect that the damn nurses felt they needed to check on me every hour. It doesn't bode well to be turned on while a nurse is hovering over you, asking how you feel."

"I thought all guys had a thing for nurses," I joked, studying his lips, which were inches away from mine.

"They have nothing on you," he said, dropping his hot open lips on mine. I whimpered against them as all the desire I'd been holding at bay since the night before roared through me like a hungry lion. Lacing my fingers through his hair, I pulled his head closer to me, unable to get enough. Sensing my need, he lifted me up in his arms so my legs were firmly wrapped around his waist. I gasped as I felt his hardness pressed up against the part of me that was throbbing with need.

"One of these days we're going to do this without any clothes," he whispered against my lips as the elevator dinged, announcing the arrival to our floor.

"And maybe we can even involve a bed," I said, unlocking my legs from around his waist as the elevator doors slid open.

Nathan groaned at my words as if he were in pain. "You're slowly killing me," he said, adjusting his pants.

I couldn't help giggling as he strolled beside me looking uncomfortable. "Fair play can be a bitch," he warned, lacing his fingers through mine.

"Ooh, I'm shaking in my boots," I mocked.

"Is that a challenge?" he asked with his eyes glinting with interest.

"Bring it on, big boy."

"Oh, it's on," he said, dragging me in for a hard kiss before helping me into his vehicle.

I was smiling at his threat as he climbed behind the wheel. I enjoyed the obvious power I had over him and was relieved it wasn't one-sided. "How about some lunch since I ripped you off at dinner last night?" he asked, backing out of the parking place.

"Can't. I have to be at Fran's by eleven," I answered, glancing at the clock on the dash, which showed the current time at a quarter past ten.

"Damn, that gives us hardly enough time to get you there, let alone stopping to get you something to eat."

"That's okay. I'm really not that hungry," I answered truthfully. My appetite was hit-or-miss lately, and it wasn't unusual for me to skip a meal or two.

"What time do you get off?"

"Six," I answered.

"You can't work for seven hours without eating anything," he said, looking disgruntled before abruptly turning the vehicle in to a fast-food restaurant right before the highway. "You can eat in the car," he insisted.

"You're kind of pushy, you know that, right?"

"I just know when I'm right," he said, pulling into the drive-through. "What would you like?" he asked as a nasal voice screeched over the intercom.

"A burger and fries is fine," I said. "Coke to drink," I added.

"Two number fours with Cokes to drink," Nathan said through his open window.

"We won't be serving lunch for another ten minutes, would you like to wait?" the voice squawked over the intercom.

Nathan looked at me questioningly. "I guess that's fine. I'll give Fran a call and tell her I'll be a few minutes late."

"We'll wait," Nathan said into the intercom.

"Pull forward, please."

Stopping in front of the drive-through window, Nathan handed over a twenty to the cashier, who looked harassed, although the day really had just started. "If you park in one of the spaces over there, we'll bring out your food when it's ready," she said, handing over our drinks and change.

"Will Fran mind that you're late?"

"No, she really only hired me to keep her company. I try to lighten her load by handling all the grunt work, but she's a tough old bird," I answered, taking a sip of my soda.

"You sound like you enjoy it," he said.

"I do. It's nice to be accountable to something that makes me feel normal," I admitted, momentarily forgetting who I was talking to. He had an easy, laid-back manner that had me disclosing information best left unsaid.

"What do you mean, normal?" he asked, taking a sip of his own drink.

"Oh, you know how life seems disjointed while you're in college. You're neither an adult out in the working world, nor a teenager who can count on your parents to solve all your problems," I lied, covering up my slip of the tongue. "It's nice to be off the limbo fence now."

"It must be hard to have lost both your parents. Do you have any other family?"

"No, it's just me," I lied again.

"That's rough," he said, eyeing me critically like he expected me to have a sudden meltdown.

I shrugged. "I try not to think about it," I said pointedly so he would change the subject.

"There's no one back home who misses you?" he persisted.

"Why? Are you changing your mind about adding my head to your collection?" I joked, hoping he'd get the hint.

He looked as if he wanted to ask me another question but must have thought better of it. "Don't you mean 'boobies in my trunk'?" he asked just as an employee from the restaurant approached his open window.

I bit off a laugh as the employee eyed us like we had two heads or something before thrusting our food at us and scurrying away. "I'm pretty sure we've traumatized her," I commented as I handed him a fry out of the bag. "You better hope she doesn't take down your license plate number."

"Wouldn't be the first time," he joked, merging onto the highway.

"I knew it all along. You're like Ted Bundy."

"You like comparing me to a serial killer, don't you?" he asked, taking the burger I had unwrapped for him.

"Well, you do fit the profile. You're good-looking, keep to yourself. No one would suspect you to be a psycho."

"No one except you, of course, Nancy Drew," he laughed.

"Whatever. Bundy was mentioned in one of my psychology classes along with some other freaky dudes."

"I took a class in college once that concentrated on the study of serial killer behaviors. It was interesting," he replied.

"You're not helping your case," I said dryly.

"Trust me, sweetheart. You'll approve of the plans I have for your body." He shot a suggestive look at me.

"You're such a flirt," I quipped, ignoring the effect his joking words had on me.

"Just keeping it real," he said seriously, taking another drink of his Coke.

"Is that right?"

"You can bank on it."

"This weather is amazing," I said, changing the subject. I rolled down my window slightly to let the cool breeze flow in.

"Truth. It's much more enjoyable running in temperatures in the low forties and fifties versus the eighties and nineties," he explained.

"I wouldn't know anything about the whole running thing, or anything involving exercise for that matter, but I agree that the lower temperatures make everything better," I said, scrunching my nose disdainfully at the idea of running.

"You don't exercise?" he asked, looking at me like I was nuts.

"God, no. Life is too short for something so disagreeable."

"Disagreeable? Now that's crazy talk. It's freeing and exhilarating. Not to mention an excellent way to clear your mind."

"I'll pass."

"What do you do to relax, then?" he asked.

"I'm active in a lot of swinger clubs," I deadpanned, laughing as he swerved slightly.

"Kidding. Right now I'm tackling a list of things I would like to try. Hence, jumping off a bridge," I answered vaguely, not delving into the title of my list.

"What else?" he asked conversationally.

"Mostly things I've never had a chance to do. Make a snow angel, a canoe ride at night, a picnic in the moonlight, a snowball fight, stuff like that. I want to do as many items on my list as I can."

"All of that sounds cool, but why the rush to do them all now? You've got your whole life ahead of you."

"Sometimes life has a way of preventing you from doing the things you want to do the most," I answered evasively.

Silence filled the car following my words. Not an uncomfortable silence, mind you. We both just sort of lapsed into our own thoughts. His presence was comforting and felt right, which sent up a warning flag in my head. Our relationship was supposed to be based on sex. Even though the sexual tension continued to hum at a low frequency between us, the tentative friendship we were forming was making its presence known.

"Favorite band?" Nathan asked, breaking the silence.

"Impossible to answer. First of all, there are too many genres I listen to, not to mention it's like asking a parent to pick a favorite child," I stated.

"Come on. You still have to have a favorite," he cajoled. "How about we narrow it down by songs?"

"That's even worse. Every song has a place and time, and it just depends on the significance they have on your life at the time. What about you?" I asked, smiling when he threw out a boy band song.

"Hey, laugh all you want, but the Backstreet Boys were good."

"You just don't seem like the Backstreet Boys type," I laughed. "Besides, I think they're like Backstreet Men now."

The rest of the ride raced by as we named off songs and the significances they held for us.

Thirty minutes later, we were debating the pros and cons of songs from the nineties, and what was currently hot on the charts, when Nathan pulled into the dirt lot on the side of

Smith's General Store. For the first time that morning, there was an uncomfortable silence between us. I wasn't sure if it was my place to mention our next hookup attempt or if he would. "So, I guess I better go in," I said, reaching for the handle.

He reached over and snagged my wrist. "I'll be here at six to pick you up," he said, pulling my hand up to his lips.

"Uh, you don't have to. I can walk home," I said, not sure about the track our relationship was currently on. I didn't sign on to get to know him. It was supposed to be sex, plain and simple.

"Like hell you can," he retorted.

"I'm wondering if we should call it quits while we're ahead. I'm not sure our possible hookup is in the cards. It's like fate is trying to give us a sign. I figure maybe we should listen. You'll only be in town for a few more days anyway," I answered, expressing my concerns.

"Are you trying to break up with me?"

"We'd have to be dating to break up," I answered.

"Fair enough. Are you trying to end our sexual exploits before they've had a chance to be explored? Are you telling me you no longer want to go bike riding with me?" he coaxed, trailing his hand over my knee.

"Of course not. I was just trying to give you an out," I said, watching his hand with bated breath as it crept higher up my leg.

"I'm not looking for an out," he said, all joking gone from his voice. "I'll be here at six to pick you up," he clarified.

"And there would be that bossy side again," I said. "You really don't have to. Maybe you should rest tonight and we can get together tomorrow," I reasoned, trying to reestablish boundaries.

"Let me get this straight. I ask you to dinner, proceed to be a total dumb-ass by eating something I'm allergic to, you rush me to the hospital, sit by my sorry ass until a room is ready and then proceed to drive forty-five minutes out of your way the next morning to pick me up, making yourself late for work, and yet you think I'd pay you back by making you walk home after stranding you at work. That's not bossy. That's owning up," he said, flipping my hand over to plant a kiss on my palm.

"Besides, I don't want to be away from you that long," he added, placing another kiss in the center of my palm.

My breath quickened at the touch of his lips. "Okay," I finally answered, forcing myself to withdraw my hand so I wouldn't be any later for work.

Shutting the car door behind me, I walked away even though I would have much rather stayed with him. I was surprised at my reluctance to leave him. Even with my pathetic experience at dating, I'd always been put off by the limited conversation skills the guys I dated seemed to have. More times than not, the conversations had been stilted and often one-sided. Usually a few hours into the date, I was ready to call it a night and anxious to escape their presence. Was this how a real relationship was supposed to be? Did people really crave the companionship of their significant other to the point of being obsessive over it?

"I'm glad to see you survived your jump," Fran greeted me as I entered the store.

"Piece of cake," I answered, donning an apron.

"Piece of cake, my ass," she grumbled, glaring at me. "You're lucky you didn't break your damn fool head."

"It might be an improvement," I quipped.

"Don't be sassy."

"Yes, ma'am," I answered, smirking.

"And don't 'ma'am' me. You know that makes me feel old," she reprimanded. "Now, tell me about your date with Mr. Handsome."

"How did you know I went out with him?" I asked, chuckling at another title being bestowed on Nathan. It seemed we could only talk about him in adjective terms.

"Darling, did you forget where you live? Plus, your man came in to ask me about restaurants. So, tell me everything. It's been years since I've heard anything spicier than Mitch Hick trying to grope Nancy Lewis during the bake sale. In her dreams, more like it."

I laughed at her words. "There's not much to tell. Nathan wound up having an allergic reaction to the cashews they put on his salad and spent the night in County General Hospital."

"Piss. Not even a kiss?" she asked, sounding highly disappointed.

"Well . . ." I hemmed and hawed, not sure how much of the kiss in my living room I was willing to share. "He may have kissed me a few times."

"Details. Now," she demanded. She perched herself on the stool behind the counter and waited for me to continue, her eyes sparkling with interest.

"We may have shared probably the hottest kiss of my exist-ence before we left for dinner last night," I admitted, blushing.

"Don't stop now," she encouraged.

"I guess you could say I was unprepared for the sensations it would evoke in me," I admitted, trying to describe it in the most tasteful way possible. Over the past few months, I'd learned that Fran was more frank than any person I'd ever known. Between her and Tressa, my sex life or lack thereof was public knowledge.

"Honey, I could have told you he'd be a good kisser. I could tell just looking at him and listening to him that he knows how to treat a woman right."

"He's such a contradiction," I admitted, sinking onto the spare stool behind the counter.

"In what way?"

"At times he seems every bit his age—sophisticated, ma-ture, in control—but when he lets his guard down, he seems years younger. It's as if he grew up too quick and forgot to have fun," I mused.

"Don't fool yourself. You're the spitting image of what you just described your young man as. It happens sometimes to those who have suffered great loss or faced circumstances no child should ever have to face," she said, looking knowingly at me.

"Are you sure you weren't a shrink in a past lifetime?" I teased.

She snorted at my words. "I could have never tolerated all the bellyaching. Now get back to the kiss and those sensations it 'evoked' in you," she said, repeating my word from earlier.

"Just put it this way: It was toe-curling, mouth-dropping, body-quivering hot."

"That's my kind of kiss. The kind where everything inside you melts away to nothing," she said, gazing out the storefront, lost in memories.

"Exactly," I agreed.

"When are you going to see him again?"

"He's picking me up after work," I admitted.

"Excellent," she said, rubbing her hands together in glee like she was the one he was picking up.

I smiled at her enthusiasm even though my own stomach was filled with butterflies. I had a good idea where Nathan and I would wind up that night, and I couldn't help being nervous about it. After our failed attempts thus far, it seemed destined that when we finally consummated our relationship, it wouldn't live up to the expectations. I couldn't help worrying that he would find me less adequate than the usual women he hooked up with. When our relationship was supposed to be a one-night stand, I at least was comforted by the idea that I wouldn't have to see him in the morning. As things stood now, I would have to face the shame if he found the sex subpar.

I was grateful that I at least had the day to gather myself. As fate would have it, though, the afternoon flew by, and before I knew it, Fran was flipping the *Open* sign over to *Closed*.

"You have fun tonight," she said to me with a glint in her eyes as I deposited her at her front door.

"Thanks," I mumbled, trying to ignore the butterflies in

my belly that couldn't have been any more active if they were completely jacked up on sugar.

Nathan was leaning against his vehicle waiting for me when I joined him. "How was your day?" he asked when I came to a stop in front of him.

"The usual. How about you?"

"Boring, but I tried to get a little work done when thoughts of you weren't intruding," he said, grinning crookedly at me. "What about you? Did you think about me at all?" he asked, pulling me closer so I stood in between the gap of his legs.

"Not at all," I lied.

"Liar," he said, using his hand to tuck my hair behind my ear. I shivered as his fingers grazed my sensitive earlobe. "I bet you thought about me as much as I thought about you," he whispered as his teeth gently nipped my ear.

"Whatever helps you sleep at night, big boy," I gasped as his mouth left a trail of heat down my neck.

"Mmm, I like the way you taste," he murmured, ignoring my taunt. He moved the collar of my shirt aside so he could rest his lips on the small indentation between my neck and collarbone. I dropped my head back, giving him free access. I didn't care that we were out in the open for the world to see. At least the setting sun cooperated by cloaking us slightly in the late-afternoon shadows.

12. *A Surprise Destination*

NATHAN

"Are you ready to go?" I asked, finally forcing myself to pull away from her delectable neck.

"Mmm-hmm," Ashton answered with her eyes still closed. She looked positively devourable standing there willing and ready in my hands. The urge to haul her to the nearest bed I could find and ravish her was almost more than I could take, but I resisted for now. I had plans for the evening that unfortunately did not include a bed until much later. It was only after I dropped her off earlier that I'd concocted the plan to give her an unforgettable evening, to make up for my complete failure the night before. I told myself it was all part of the whole seduction plan. Charm her, screw her, and then hand her over. The problem was everything felt different now. I'd never allowed myself to become emotionally attached on a job, but Ashton was no ordinary mark. I wasn't sure if my elaborate plans for the evening were nothing more than a way to ease my guilty conscience.

Everything had come together relatively easy thanks to a few kind townsfolk and one of her best friends who had been very accommodating with my requests. By the end of the evening, Ashton would be putty in my hands, and I would finally be able to get her out of my system. As long as the weather held together, the night would be perfect. Unfortunately, my patience was being tested by low heavy clouds that had moved in over the horizon as the day progressed.

"We better head out," I said, dropping a quick kiss on each of her closed eyelids. "Hopefully, the weather cooperates," I added.

"Why, where are we going?" she asked, slightly confused. Her eyes were still cloudy with passion that tested my already shaky restraint. "I thought we were going back to my place," she added, sounding disappointed.

"I have something else planned," I answered, smiling at her disappointment.

"Oh, okay. Where are we going then?" she repeated.

"You'll have to wait and see," I said, dropping my voice so it would come out mysterious. I placed my finger against her lips when she tried to say something else. "It's a surprise."

"I hate surprises," she griped, climbing into the passenger seat.

"You're a chick, how can you hate surprises?"

"Because you never know what's going to happen."

"Hence the word *surprise*," I teased.

"Why don't you tell me, and then I'll act surprised," she cajoled.

"Um, how about *not*," I answered, pulling onto the dirt road I had driven down just a few hours prior.

"I think you took a wrong turn. I'm pretty sure this road belongs to Mr. James and doesn't lead anywhere," she piped in as I continued to drive slowly over the ruts in the road, trying to avoid the tree branches on either side of the narrow lane.

"It's all good," I reassured her, lacing my fingers through hers.

"Oh shit, this is the time when you're finally going to add my boobies to your trunk."

"You got me. Surprise," I teased.

The trees surrounding the vehicle closed in tighter around us, scraping against the sides of the Range Rover in one last-ditch attempt to keep us out before opening up to a clearing with a large lake bordering the property. Ashton gasped beside me when she took in the sight in front of us. I had to admit, we'd done a great job creating the effect I wanted. The clearing was illuminated by multiple lanterns that hung from the low branches of the towering trees. Candles sat on the ground, flickering in vases, and surrounded a large quilt that had been spread out on the ground. I smiled at the overall effect. Ashton's friend Tressa had outdone herself.

I'd been hesitant to employ her help, afraid she'd tip Ashton off on the surprise, but she'd proved to be a godsend. She jumped in wholeheartedly at the chance to help me surprise Ashton. Her ideas were sound, and I let her run with them.

"The clouds kind of screwed up my whole plan for a picnic beneath the moon, but you get the idea," I said proudly.

"What are you trying to do to me?" Ashton asked, looking awestruck at the scene before us.

"I figured I owed you for last night," I said, linking my fingers through hers so I could drag her to the waiting blanket and picnic basket perched on top of it. "This way we can knock two of those items off that list you have," I added as she looked completely transfixed by the lanterns.

"Two?" she asked with a catch in her voice.

"A canoe ride beneath the stars," I answered, pointing to the aluminum canoe I'd finally been able to track down. "I'm hoping the clouds will give us a break," I added wryly.

"This is too much," Ashton said, not looking ecstatic like I had pictured she would be.

"What do you mean, sweetheart?" I asked, placing my hands on her shoulders.

She shrugged them off. "This," she said, pointing to the picnic. "And that," she added, pointing to the canoe.

"Why is it too much?" I asked, confused. Sure, I might have gone a little overboard for this date, but the end result would make it all worth it. Somewhere between deciding not to turn her over to my client right away and making her mine, I decided I wanted to get to know her better. I wanted to know why she had run. I had to know why her eyes occasionally clouded over with hopelessness, and what lurked behind the passion that flared up in those same eyes. She was like a rare treasure that begged to be discovered and explored.

"Because we're not a couple," she said. "We're not even lovers yet," she added through gritted teeth before turning and stalking off for the vehicle.

"Hey, wait. I know we're not," I said, snagging her hand after she'd taken only a few steps. "But that doesn't mean we can't get to know each other and enjoy the time we have together," I said, cupping her face with my hands. "I just want to enhance what we have going on here."

"You're trying to make me fall in love with you," she said with trembling lips. She looked as if she were fighting back tears.

"I've already been down the heartbreak route and have no plans to travel it ever again, but that doesn't mean I'm not going to enjoy what we have going on here. You yourself have to admit that the connection between us is more than lust," I said, pulling her closer. "I say let's explore it and just enjoy it. There's no reason we need to rush any of this. We can let the anticipation build up before we finally let it crash over us. I've taken the next few weeks off from work. Spend them with me," I pleaded.

"This was supposed to be just an affair," she said, her eyes shining bright with unshed tears.

"And that's what it will be. That doesn't mean we can't have fun discovering each other along the way."

"What if you fall in love with me?"

"You keep asking that. Trust me on this. My heart is too hardened to ever love again," I said, running my hand up the side of her face. Pulling her close, I placed my lips to hers, probing with my tongue until she opened her mouth fully. Our lips caressed each other until the rigidness in her arms disappeared and she melted against me. "Tell me you'll spend the next few weeks with me," I said, pulling back despite her protests.

Her answer was a small nod before she brought my mouth back to hers.

13. *Caught in the Rain*

ASHTON

I was a goner. I knew it the moment we pulled into the clearing and I saw what he had done. Unintentionally or not, he was slowly chipping away at my resolve to treat our relationship casually. It was if he saw through my carefree façade where I contemplated one-night stands and treated affairs like I was ordering dessert. Somehow he had figured out I wasn't that kind of person. He was offering to take it slow, and obviously planned on wooing me if the scene before me was any indication. It was like a fairy tale. What girl didn't dream about a candle-filled evening with a man who made her pulse race and her heart skip a beat? The problem was I shouldn't want any of it. More accurately, I shouldn't be allowed to want it. I tried to leave, but somehow, standing in Nathan's arms with him begging me to stay with him for a few weeks crumbled my resolve.

"Let's eat," Nathan finally said, breaking the kiss.

"Okay," I answered, letting him lead me to the heavy quilt that was stretched on the ground in front of us. I sat down and watched as he unpacked the large picnic basket, doing my best to hide my surprise when each new item he pulled from the basket seemed to be a favorite of mine. There were chocolate-covered strawberries from Haley's Delectable Eats bakery, several varieties of cheeses and crackers, artichoke dip and pita slices, and a bottle of my favorite wine.

"You did your homework," I said, trying for blasé. I didn't want to admit what his attention to detail meant to me.

"I may have had help," he chuckled, popping the cork off the wine and pouring me a glass.

"I suspected as much," I said, sweeping my eyes around. "Tressa?"

"That would be the one. She jumped at the chance to help me out."

"I bet she did," I said, smirking at him.

He laughed. "She's a character, for sure. I don't think she has a shy bone in her body. I got the whole lowdown on her ex and the new guy she's going out with this weekend," he said wryly, shoving a cracker in his mouth.

I laughed. "Yeah, Tressa's not shy by a long shot. And her ex is a total douche," I added.

"He sounds like it, and his mom doesn't sound like much of a winner either. I'm not sure what I would have done at his age if my mom tried to cockblock me," he said just as I was taking a sip of wine. His words made the wine go down the wrong tube and I choked, nearly covering him in a combination of wine and spit.

Nathan pounded me on the back as I coughed like an eighty-year-old smoker. "Not cool to say something like that when I'm trying to drink," I chastised in between coughs. "You gotta give a person warning."

"Sorry," he said, laughing again. "Anyway, your friend is better off now. At least I think so."

"That's what I told her. We've all gone out together a couple of times and he was always very overbearing where she was concerned. It irked me that he kept such a tight rein on her. No girl deserves to be treated that way."

"You sound like you have personal experience in that area?" he asked casually, though I sensed something more in his tone.

"Me? Hell no," I said, reaching for a chocolate strawberry. "I may have not dated much, but I'd never let a guy treat me like that. If anyone tried to control me like Jackson did with Tressa, I would have sent him packing instantly," I added, looking up at him. I was surprised to see that his eyes had narrowed and he was studying me critically. I instantly regretted my openness. He didn't need to hear about my love life or lack thereof. It was as if I had erected a flashing sign above my head with the word *inexperienced* in big red letters for the world to see.

The silence between us stretched on as he moved his eyes from mine and studied the water behind me. I had the uncomfortable feeling he was contemplating what he was doing with someone with my adolescent experience. Maybe we had reached the point where he was missing the sophisticated and experienced ladies he was used to dating. I felt I should say something. Offer up some kind of reassurance that I wasn't a complete prude or anything, but I kept my lips sealed, waiting for him to break the silence.

After what seemed like an eternity, he finally shifted his eyes back to me. "So, you've never been in a relationship you couldn't wait to get out of?" he asked with intensity.

"No," I answered, puzzled. I knew the fact that I was twenty-two and had no prior experience to brag about could be construed as unusual, but it shouldn't put me on trial. "It's not like I'm a leper or something," I finally said sarcastically, done with the way he was looking at me.

"Of course not," he answered. "It's just unusual that you don't have one crummy relationship to complain about."

"What the hell does that mean? Maybe I was too busy to have a real relationship. Maybe my sights were focused on finishing college early, so I didn't invest much time in dating," I answered truthfully. Not to mention that for the longest time my only goal was to make up for the year I was forced to repeat in high school. Watching my fellow classmates graduate without me had been a tough pill to swallow, so I made it my goal to get my college degree as fast as I could. Free time became a novelty once I entered college and submerged myself in as many classes as my counselor was willing to allow me to take. Even summers merged together with the rest of the school year as I pushed on without taking any breaks. I went year-round with the goal of graduating a year early. My hard work paid off too. Three years after graduating from high school I had my bachelor's degree in hand, but by then it didn't matter.

"I see," Nathan said, interrupting my thoughts.

"Why is it such a bad thing that I've never had my heart broken?" I asked, sick of the way he was acting.

"It's not," he answered, reaching for my hand. "It just surprised me," he added, smiling at me.

"What about you? Who broke your heart?" I probed.

"What makes you think my heart's been broken?"

"Well, the way you're acting, for one. Besides that, you've mentioned going down the heartbreak route a couple times," I said, studying his features, which had gone hard in the flickering candlelight. "If it makes you uncomfortable, you don't have to talk about it," I said quietly.

"Her name was Jessica Swanson, and she came into my life like a freaking hurricane. She was no-nonsense and bossy as hell. In the beginning, I was flattered that she picked me the night I met her at a school play. She put me together, you know? Made me grow up and taught me to take my future seriously. I guess you could say she groomed me. After we'd been dating for several months, I found out her family was swimming in the bucks. It was a world I didn't belong in, but I didn't care. I fooled myself into thinking I loved her. The first time I met her family was hell. Her father drilled me for hours about my future plans. That's when I realized why Jessica had been pushing me so hard. In her family, it was all about who you knew, how to make it to the top, and who you were willing to step on to get there," he said in a pained voice. He remained silent for a moment, and I was beginning to think he was done when he started talking again. "It took me almost a year to realize just how far Jessica was willing to go to ensure my future. I mean crazy shit you couldn't even imagine. I caught her in bed with a congressman twice her age. A fucking congressman. Can you imagine that shit? She had some crazy-ass high hopes that I would have a career in politics or something, and this was how she would help get me there. That's how she justified it, as fucked up as that sounds."

"That is seriously fucked up," I said, understanding his hang-ups on love.

His eyes were expressionless in the flickering light of the candles, making it hard for me to tell what he was thinking. After a few long silence-filled minutes, he surprised me by changing the subject completely.

"What college did you go to?" he asked, sounding normal again.

"The University of Central Florida. What about you?" I asked, glad the weirdness between us was dissipating.

"FSU," he answered. "Of course, several years before you were in college," he added.

"Right. I was, like, in middle school when you were in college," I said, laughing as he grimaced.

"That just sounds wrong. Maybe we'll leave that fact out from now on," he said as the rest of the tension evaporated.

"I thought all guys wanted to hook up with a younger girl," I quipped, nibbling on another chocolate strawberry.

"True. We just don't like to talk about the ages, at least our ages. As for the girl, we'd put it on a billboard if it made us look better," he said, looking at me appraisingly. "Are you trying to drive me mad?" he added, watching me lick the corner of my mouth, where a small piece of chocolate threatened to escape.

"By eating a strawberry?" I inquired as a thrill of excitement raced through me at the way he was eyeing me.

"Eating is one thing. I mean the way your mouth seems to cherish every bite. That's driving me insane. I've never been jealous of a fruit before."

"I can't help it. They're so good, mmm," I moaned, opening my mouth wide to take in the entire piece of fruit. He sat watching me for a moment as I laughed. Finally, he leaned over and pulled me against him, capturing my lips with his. I gasped with approval when his tongue swept into my mouth. My desire flared up instantly, making me grasp at his shirt like a drowning victim. I submerged myself in the kiss as if it were my only source for life. His passion seemed to match mine as he tangled his hands in my hair, pulling me as close as we could get. The remnants of our dinner were forgotten as he lowered himself on the quilt with me sprawled on top of him without breaking the kiss. Every inch of me wanted him now. I strained against him, unsure how to tell him what I wanted as my need for something more became unbearable.

"You were right, it did taste so good," he finally said, breathing heavily as he broke the kiss and sat back up, cradling me in his arms. I bit back my disappointment that he'd broken the kiss. Maybe he didn't enjoy it as much as I did. Of course, when he shifted me in his arms and my bottom sank more intimately in his lap, I could feel every hard inch of him pressed against me, letting me know just how much the kiss had affected him.

"Would you like another taste?" I asked brazenly, popping a smaller strawberry in my mouth. I was going for seductive, but the strawberry turned out to be juicier than I expected. Red juice squirted out of my mouth in the least seductive way imaginable, squirting him square in the face. "Oops," I said, reaching out to wipe the juice off his face, fighting the urge to giggle.

"Delicious," he said, licking a droplet off his lips, gaining my full attention again. Maybe I was biased since I'd already witnessed firsthand how they felt, but his lips were possibly the most erotic lips I'd ever seen. They were full and plush and every bit as soft as they looked, but had the potential to turn hard when you most wanted them to. Leaning toward him, I placed my lips on his and used the tip of my tongue to remove the last of the strawberry juice. I wanted to explore his mouth with my tongue. He groaned and in one fluid movement maneuvered me so I was straddling him. His hands found my hips and pulled me snugly against the hardness in his pants. I felt powerful from the way his body reacted to my touch. He gave me free rein over him as I thrust my tongue into his mouth. The ache between my legs hit an all-time high. He swallowed my moan of pleasure, using his hands to guide my hips where he wanted me. My breaths came out in shallow pants as his hand crept under my layers of clothing and reached bare skin. Slowly, he caressed his way up my back, feeling the heat of my passion. I moaned again as he moved from around my back to the swells of my breasts, waiting with bated breath as he lightly played with the lace of my bra before withdrawing.

"It's time for part two of our date," he said, pulling back.

"You asshole. I thought this was part two," I said, rubbing up against him to emphasize my point.

His eyes closed briefly. "I'm beginning to think you'll be the death of me."

"It's your own fault," I breathed into his ear.

"I'm trying to show you a proper date, and all I can think about is burying myself in you."

"Proper is boring," I commented, shifting again.

"Damn, woman," he groaned, pulling my hips hard against him one last time before abruptly lifting me off his lap. Hopping to his feet, he pulled me up with him. "Phase two of the date," he stated, dragging me toward the canoe on the shore.

"Where's the fire?" I complained, trying to clear the fog out of my head his kisses had caused.

"Burning out of control inside me. If I didn't get you away from the blanket, it was go time," he stated.

"I thought that's what we were here for," I piped in, looking back at the blanket longingly.

"I'm aware of that," he said, shooting me a wry look as he pushed the canoe to the water's edge. "Hop in," he told me, holding the canoe in place.

"I'd rather go back to the blanket." I pouted, looking over my shoulder at the blanket one last time.

"Get in," he mock-growled, making me laugh.

Stepping into the canoe, I braced my legs, trying to gain my balance from the swaying beneath me. When it finally stopped rocking from my weight, I sat on one of the narrow metal benches.

"Here," Nathan said, handing the two oars to me before climbing into the canoe. The canoe rocked dangerously from his weight before settling back down. Sitting on the bench opposite from me, Nathan reached out for one of the oars. He used it for leverage, pushing against the bank of the lake until the aluminum canoe moved off the sand that was holding us in place. Once we were adrift, he reached for the other oar. He made short work of rowing us away from the shore.

I leaned my head back, wishing the thick heavy clouds weren't obstructing the moon and stars. I had to admit, though, the clouds gave off a different allure that was beautiful in its own way. It was as if we were floating off into some mysterious void, shrouded in darkness and haze. When I had added this moment to my list, I always imagined something breathtaking, but the weather today made this something more. I could have stared at the big puffy clouds all night if not for the fact that the breeze blowing off the water was chilling me to the bone. A violent shiver trembled through me as one of the gusts sliced through my clothing.

"Come over here," Nathan said, indicating the floor of the canoe between his legs, where he'd stacked a couple of life jackets for me to perch on.

I moved cautiously so I wouldn't tip the canoe. With his help, I sank down on the life jackets between his legs and felt warmer almost instantly. I leaned back against him, resting my head on his chest so I could look at the sky again.

"The clouds look amazing," I murmured.

"Very," he answered, trailing a hand across my cheek. I tilted my head and saw that he wasn't talking about the sky like I was. He cupped my face gently in his hands, holding it in place. My breath hitched in my lungs as he leaned in to drop a soft kiss on my lips. Whereas the other kisses we had shared ignited the lust we felt for each other, this kiss was something entirely different. The softness of his lips caressed mine as his tongue slowly slid into my mouth. He explored my mouth leisurely, never increasing the intensity. It was as if he were trying to memorize every detail and was meticulous with his mission. The tenderness of his mouth made my heart ache and I wished it would never end. That is, until a large drop of water landed on my cheek, quickly followed by another, and then another.

"Oh hell," he said, pulling back as the sky opened up above us.

"Holy crap!" I said as the freezing rain found its way down the back of my jacket and into my shirt.

Nathan grabbed the oars and dug them into the water to propel us back to shore, but the distance seemed insanely far. We were going to be soaked no matter what. I scooted back to my seat, taking care not to capsize the boat and add to our dilemma.

14. *Shower for Two*

NATHAN

There's a time in everyone's life when I'm sure they wonder if fate is actually some dude watching from beyond, just waiting for the right moment to fuck with us. Feeling the first raindrops land on my head as I was bent over enjoying Ashton's lips made me believe this was one of those times. Having the sky dump on us out of nowhere convinced me he was one sick bastard.

Watching Ashton huddled on the small metal seat, trying to stay warm as the rain continued to pelt us, made me feel like the biggest asshole ever. I was zero for two now in the dating game.

A giant shiver rippled through Ashton's delicate frame. I dug into the oars with all my strength, but these damn metal canoes only move so fast through the water. The rain made the oars slippery and my hands quickly became blocks of ice, but I ignored the physical discomfort and drove us forward. I had one goal: Get to the shore so we could get out of the icy rain as soon as possible.

By the time the canoe hit the sandy embankment, the rain was falling in sheets around us, making it hard to see. Our clothes were plastered to our skin, freezing us to the bone. I grabbed Ashton's freezing hand to haul her ashore. We were both shaking uncontrollably from the cold.

Still holding her hand, we raced toward my Range Rover, not taking into consideration the muddy ground that was slick as oil under our feet. One moment I was standing upright with my destination only steps away, and the next I was flat on my back as the rain continued to pelt my face. Ashton, who had been clutching my hand, stood above me shaking with cold and laughter.

"You think this is funny?" I asked, tugging her hand and setting her flat on her ass next to me.

Her eyes were filled with mirth despite the fact that we were both freezing our asses off and covered in mud. "Is this phase three of the date, to make mud pies?" she asked. Before I could answer, she plastered a handful of mud across my face.

"Oh, it's on now, baby," I said, grabbing her ankles as she attempted to scramble away. "Welcome to the spa, madam, your mud bath is ready."

"Gah, no," she laughed, and she squirmed as I made quick work of covering her. We wrestled around on the wet ground, looking like two pigs covered in slop by the time we were done.

Despite the driving rain and the fact I was freezing my nuts off, I couldn't help joining in her laughter. We were both soaking wet and covered from head to toe in mud. She looked enticing as hell despite the circumstances. Perhaps it was the fact that she could laugh through it all, but at that moment, I wanted to haul her into my arms and never let go. I was finally forced to act like a sane adult, though, when her laughter and shivers made it impossible for her to stand up. Without giving her a chance to protest, I swept her up in my arms and hoisted her over my shoulder as I cautiously carried her to the Range Rover. She was still giggling as I deposited her shaking body in the passenger seat before hurrying around to the driver's side. My feet threatened to come out from under me again as I was rounding the back of the vehicle, but I was able to keep myself upright by holding on. I was swearing by the time I climbed behind the steering wheel, which made Ashton laugh harder.

"Chuckle it up. It's not like you were any more graceful," I mock-growled. My fingers were doing their best not to co-operate as I fumbled to slide the key into the ignition. Finally, after several attempts, I was able to crank the vehicle over and turn the heat to the highest setting. The air blasted out at us and rose quickly in temperature. We both felt instant relief. I let the vehicle warm up for a few more minutes before finally turning around and driving away from the clearing.

"You better hope we don't get pulled over," Ashton giggled through her knocking teeth as I pulled onto the main road.

I laughed, relieved that she was feeling good enough to joke. "Why?"

"Because they may think we're into some kinky mud-wrestling thing."

"Mud wrestling? Is that the kind of thing you like?" I teased.

"Oh yeah. No weekend was complete at UCF until I was in some kind of mud pit," she said dryly.

"You, skimpy outfit, mud—that's something I'd like to see," I said, winking at her.

"Spoken like a true male," she said as I pulled into her driveway. "I think I'll just stay in the car with the heat," she added, not thrilled about going outside again.

"We'll be inside before you know it," I reassured her. "Where are your keys?"

"In my purse," she answered, leaning down to pick it up. Digging around for a few seconds, she finally found them and handed them over.

I reached over after turning off the vehicle and popped the glove compartment to pull out the box I had placed in there earlier.

The wide-eyed look on Ashton's face was hilarious when she saw the box of condoms in my hand. Smiling, I opened my door and almost changed my mind when a freezing gust of wind swept into the vehicle. "Holy shit, it's colder than a witch's tit out here," I complained, grimacing as the rain drove down on me. I continued to curse as I rounded the vehicle only to find Ashton already headed toward her front door.

"I would have carried you," I said as she bounced from one foot to the other.

"It's okay," she said, shivering.

I unlocked the front door as quick as I could and propelled her inside. Unfortunately, it wasn't much warmer in the cottage than it was outside. "Where's the thermostat?" I asked as she stood in the center of the room shaking from head to toe.

"My room."

I bumped up the heat until I heard it kick on and then dropped the small box on her nightstand before proceeding to the bathroom. I got a hot shower started before going back out to collect Ashton.

She was right where I had left her, still shaking like a leaf on a windy day. "Come on," I said, pulling her toward the bathroom. A wall of steam greeted us when I opened the door. The warmth draped our cold bodies like a blanket. Ashton's eyes were heavy with exhaustion from the night's events. She was leaning heavily against the closed bathroom door and looked ready to drop.

"Take off your clothes," I said as I pulled at my own clothes with numb fingers.

"I'm really not in the mood," she joked. Her lips were a pale blue and her frame was shaking out of control.

"Very funny," I said, reaching out to help her when I saw the cold had rendered her fingers useless. I stripped off her muddy sweater and the long-sleeved T-shirt she had on underneath and then deftly unfastened the button of her jeans.

"I can do it," she said, standing in her bra and jeans in front of me with teeth knocking together.

I pulled off my own muddy jeans as she struggled to remove her own. Finally, after a few false attempts, she stood before me, pale but beautiful in only her delicate lace bra and her barely-there panties. Had we not been frozen and blue from the cold, I could have stared at her forever without ever tiring.

"I knew you were a boxer-briefs kind of guy," she said in an exhausted voice as I stood in front of her.

"I'm going to get you in the hot shower to warm you up and then you can sleep," I said, pulling her toward the shower as I followed behind. As we stepped into the shower together, I adjusted the setting so we wouldn't be scalded and then pulled her into my arms under the cascading flow of water. The shaking of her body seemed to intensify for a moment before she sagged against me, sighing as the warmth began to penetrate her freezing limbs. I turned her against me so she could hold on without falling. I lost track of how long we stood under the stream of hot water. Before the temperature of the water could change, I finally forced myself to move. Reaching behind her, I unclasped her bra and pulled back slightly so the straps could slip off her arms. I willed myself to not look, but I couldn't help sweeping my eyes down her body, taking in her puckered perky nipples before crushing her back against me. Controlling my body's reaction to holding her topless form was a mammoth task that I was failing at miserably. She was practically asleep on her feet, which made my arousal seem almost dirty. Feeling slightly embarrassed, I finally looked down to see if she was aware of my response. I was shocked to find her looking at me with full awareness. I smiled apologetically. "Sorry," I said, no longer able to hide the evidence of my desire pressed against her.

"For what?" she asked, leaning forward to lick a bead of water off my collarbone.

"For wanting you this badly during a pretty shitty time."

"So we took a boat ride in the rain and froze our asses off. The before and definitely the after make up for it," she said as I squeezed soap onto the washcloth. Keeping my eyes on hers, I slowly began to wash the last traces of mud from her body.

"I'm not sure those were muddy," she said in a hitched voice when I ran the washcloth over her breasts.

"Just trying to be thorough," I said before dropping a kiss to her shoulder blade.

"Hmmmm, thorough. Well, who am I to argue?" she said, reaching up to link her arms around my neck. The movement brought her breasts flush against my chest. I bent my head and dropped a kiss to her other shoulder.

"The water's starting to cool," I said regretfully, twisting the nozzle until the flow of water stopped. I reached around the curtain and grabbed a large towel off the rack and wrapped it around her. Without breaking eye contact, I hooked my fingers on either side of her panties, pulling them down her hips until they rested at her feet, where she was able to step out of them. Her eyes stayed on mine as I pulled off my own boxer-briefs before reaching for a towel. Steamy air crept into the hallway when I opened the bathroom door. The hardwood floors were still cold on bare feet for the walk to her bedroom, but at least the heater had sufficiently warmed up the cottage while we showered. I pulled down the heavy comforter on her bed and turned back to Ashton, who was watching me intently. Our eyes remained locked, neither of us saying a word. I grabbed the towel she held in place around her body and paused. She waited for a moment as the intensity of our stare reached a boiling point before raising her arms, allowing the towel to drop to the floor. I allowed myself the luxury of looking at her fully naked body for the first time. Every inch of her skin begged for my touch, and I was no longer able to help myself. I gently massaged one of her perfectly sculpted breasts before dropping a quick kiss just above her erect nipple.

"That was nice," she said, finally breaking the silence and making me stand on end.

15. *Finally, a Night to Remember*

ASHTON

My body was ready and there would be no stopping this time. Nathan and I stood facing each other as his hands moved gently over my skin, making me tingle. He continued down my arms before lifting my hands to his chest. I matched his movements, using my fingertips to trace the contours of his firm pectorals. We were almost dancing now as I continued down with my fingers to his gloriously chiseled abs. My eyes followed a single drop of water, traveling along the grooves of his muscular stomach and then down to his fully erect member below. Seeing it for the first time only heightened my arousal. The familiar ache between my legs spread quickly from our movements, making me yearn for more. I moved close against him, moaning with delight when he placed his mouth on my neck. He moved along my shoulder with his lips and up to my ear.

"You like that?" he asked, moaning himself from my enthusiastic approval. Turning me slowly around, he continued kissing along my back before pulling me tightly against him. His hands cupped my breasts as he swayed slowly against my ass, sending liquid heat rushing throughout my body.

"God," I moaned, turning around and pulling him toward the bed. "Put it in now. I need you."

"I know, baby. I need you too, but trust me. I'm going to give you the best bike ride ever," he answered, lowering me down to the bed.

He draped himself on top of me, kissing down my chest and using his tongue along my nipple before taking it all in his mouth. I decided instantly I loved being sucked like that and wanted more. With bated breath, I silently begged him to move lower, which of course he obliged.

"You mean, here?" He kissed my stomach. "Or here?" he repeated, going slightly lower.

Passion consumed me. I moved against him, wanting more but unsure how to convey what I needed. My breath became labored as he moved his hand lower. I parted my legs, allowing his hand access to where I needed it. He rubbed his fingers intimately against me. The sensation was unlike any I had ever felt. My hips rose, almost instinctively on their own, and my movements became frantic as he continued to rub his fingers against me. I felt as if I were reaching the crest of a gigantic wave. As my senses reached the point of eruption, I felt his tongue tickling the spot where his fingers had been, making me buck against him as spasms took over my body.

I was slowly coming back down to earth when he finally spoke.

"You're trying to kill me, aren't you?" he said, slowly withdrawing before lying on me again.

"And why is that?" I asked when I could speak again.

"Because everything you do is so fucking hot. It was turning me on as much to watch you as it was to do it to you," he answered, running his hand up my torso until it grazed over my breast. He dropped his mouth to mine without saying another word. His desire was apparent as his tongue made love to my mouth, moving in and out and making my body respond again. I could feel him hot and hard against my thigh and I shifted again, hoping he'd get the hint of where I wanted him the most.

"We're getting there, sweetheart," he said, dragging his lips from mine and trailing them down my collarbone until his mouth closed fully around my nipple.

"Give me a second," he said, reaching over for the box he'd left on my table earlier. I shifted against him, ready to feel him inside me as he extracted a condom from its package.

His mouth found my ear as he settled between my legs again. "Tell me what you want," he whispered huskily.

"I want you," I said, unsure how to tell him exactly what I wanted.

"Where?" he breathed, pulling my earlobe into his mouth, making me buck beneath him.

"There," I said, lifting my hips for emphasis.

"Here?" he nudged, moving my legs farther apart so he could settle fully against me.

"Yes," I moaned as he slid inside me.

"God, you feel so fucking good," he said, straining as he moved slowly in me.

Unable to take the torture anymore, I raised my hips, taking him fully. My fingers raked hard against his back, pulling him against me. He lost all self-control as our bodies moved together. His lips found mine through labored breathing, and I could feel the wave building as he called out my name.

"Oh, Ashton, fuck," he called, moving faster and faster. My body felt like it would explode until we reached the climax, finishing together.

I felt completely spent with all my limbs like jelly. "Holy crap, is it always like that?" I asked as he rested heavily on top of me.

"It's never been like that," he answered, propping himself on an elbow.

"Really? You're not just trying to make me feel good?"

"Really," he answered, dropping a light kiss on my lips before rising off me and heading for my bathroom.

A few minutes later, Nathan returned and switched off the light before climbing into bed. I tucked myself under his arm, sighing with satisfaction as he stroked my hair. I flushed slightly, remembering how I had responded so completely to his touch. I had been unprepared for how consuming making love was and how everything else of importance melted away. All I could focus on now was how badly I wanted him to keep touching me.

16. *The Pledge*

NATHAN

"Sleep," I said, when she shifted her hips in my direction.

"Not likely," she breathed.

"You're exhausted. You'll be asleep before you know it. Just relax," I coaxed.

She shifted again and I tightened my hold on her.

"I'm not all that tired. We could if you wanted," she whispered in the dark. I might have taken her up on it if not for the stifled yawn I heard from her.

"Sweetheart, when we go again, I want you to be completely alert. Now, go to sleep," I encouraged.

I thought she was going to argue more, but she relaxed against me. "Thank you for an unforgettable night," she said.

I chuckled. "Anytime. Thank you for being you."

"Mmm-hmm," she said as sleep dragged her under.

A moment later, her body fell completely relaxed in my arms, letting me know she was out. I was still filled with a little too much adrenaline to sleep. Of course, it wasn't much of a hardship to hold her slender body in my arms, and I didn't mind being awake for it. She was equally beautiful in her sleep and by far the most engaging woman I had ever been with, making all others pale in comparison. Her quick wit and honesty on most issues pulled me in, making me want to learn everything about her. I couldn't help wishing she would trust me enough to confide her secrets. Her lies about never having a serious relationship had bothered me more than I had expected. I knew my response had confused her as I had fought to control my anger. The fact that she felt she had to lie made me want to hunt my employer down and beat him to a bloody pulp. What had he done to her to make her want to run away? I lay there for what felt like hours pondering several scenarios through my head, trying to make sense of why she was hiding the truth. Finally, my own exhaustion got the better of me, and I gave up trying to solve the mystery for the night. My last coherent thought before I succumbed to sleep was that it would be a cold day in hell before I allowed anyone to hurt her again.

17. *The Next Day*

ASHTON

I woke the next morning to the sound of my front door opening. Seeing I was alone, I sprang from my bed like someone had set off a firecracker. Everything we did last night was great, but hanging out in my birthday suit in broad daylight was a whole other issue. I hurried to throw on a pair of yoga pants and a cream-colored T-shirt when Nathan walked in. As per usual, hurrying never worked out in my favor, as evidenced by my head stuck halfway through one of the sleeves of the shirt and my inside-out and backward yoga pants.

"New fashion statement?" he asked, holding a bag from the bakery in his hand.

I glared at him through the opening of my T-shirt sleeve as I tried in vain to pull the hem of the shirt down to cover my exposed chest.

"Here, let me help," he said, setting the bag down on top of my dresser.

"I got it," I said, backing away in embarrassment, but of course I misjudged the distance between my bed and me and wound up falling backward onto my bed in an unceremonious heap. Well, at least it wasn't anything he hadn't seen before. Ironically, I'd never been a klutz prior to meeting him. It was as if my brain didn't transmit the appropriate messages to my limbs when he was around.

"You sure?" he asked, suppressing a laugh. "You know, darling, there's nothing to be embarrassed about," he added, sitting on the bed beside me. "If it helps, last night was one of the most erotic nights of my life," he said, running a hand over my bare stomach.

"It was?" I squeaked out, finally finding the neck of my shirt.

"Was it for you?" he asked seriously, letting his fingers trail up over my rib cage.

"Of course," I answered eagerly without hesitation. Although I was sure I should have been acting like it was no big deal. "It was nice," I added lamely.

"Nice?" he asked, bending over to kiss my stomach.

"Really nice," I murmured as his lips skimmed over my belly button before dipping lower.

"Not erotic?" he asked, running his tongue along the skin just above the top of my pants.

"Yes, it was erotic," I gasped as his tongue found its way beneath my pants.

"The most erotic?" he coaxed, pulling my pants down slightly.

"The most," I agreed as he ran his tongue up the length of my torso.

"Fantastic," he said, hiking up my pants and hauling me to my feet in one fluid movement. "We'll have to explore that later. I have plans for us today," he said, giving my bottom a slight shove toward my bathroom. "Get ready, daylight's a-wasting," he added.

"What?" I sputtered, confused how in the span of a moment we'd gone from a talk about what was erotic to being hauled to my feet and being told to get ready.

"You told me you'd spend a few weeks with me, so I've made some plans," he said with a devilish grin.

"How do you know I don't have to work?" I asked, placing my hands on my hips.

"I checked with Fran when I dropped off her picnic basket. She was kind enough to tell me your days off."

"Her picnic basket?" I asked. "I'm not surprised. That explains her behavior yesterday. She looked like she'd swallowed a canary most of the day," I added.

"She's been extremely helpful."

"I bet. Where else did you go this morning?"

"I went to get the stuff we left after our late-night picnic. I figured I'd beat Mr. James to his property so he wouldn't see the mess we left behind."

"Did you beat him?" I asked in a small voice, just imagining what conclusions someone would jump to when they saw the remains of our evening.

"Funny enough, I didn't know that Mr. James likes to fish on his property every morning. According to him, 'the early bird gets the worm.'"

"Oh, God," I mumbled. "Well, everyone knows now," I said, sagging against the bathroom doorway.

"And that's bad?" he asked, approaching me and placing his hands on my hips.

"People will talk," I said.

"Most people do. That's why we have tongues," he teased. "Does it bother you that it's with me, or just that people will know we had sex?"

"The sex," I said, trying not to blush. "For fuck's sake. I'm twenty-two and acting like *sex* is a bad word."

"Honey, we're two consenting adults. They can say whatever they want," he said, dropping a kiss on my jaw. "Now, hurry and get ready," he bossed, shooing me through the bathroom door.

"You're not the boss of me," I muttered, closing the door in his face. "I'll take as long as I want," I called through the door for good measure. I could hear him chuckling as he headed out of my room. Despite my arguments, I hurried through my morning rituals. My hair was thrown up on top of my head in a messy bun and my makeup was kept to a minimum with just eyeliner and a light layer of foundation. The only task I didn't rush through was brushing my teeth. Brushing them once didn't seem sufficient, so I proceeded to brush them again after I had flossed and rinsed my mouth with mouthwash. Running my tongue over my squeaky-clean teeth,

I smiled in satisfaction before smoothing on a layer of lip gloss.

Five minutes later, I left my room dressed in another heavy sweater and a pair of skinny jeans.

Nathan was in the process of taking a sip of coffee when I entered the living room. He froze with the cup halfway to his lips, studying me intensely.

"What?" I asked, doing a quick check to make sure my zipper was up and that my hair wasn't suddenly standing on end.

He didn't answer, but instead walked over to where I stood.

"You didn't say where we were going, so I figured casual was the best route . . ." I trailed off as he cupped a hand around my neck and dragged my mouth to his. I opened my mouth to his demands, not sure what the kiss meant. If it was possible, the kiss felt different than the others we had shared. It felt raw and almost primal as he assaulted my mouth. My body's response was quick and instantaneous.

"What was that?" I asked when he finally pulled back, breathing heavily.

"That was my way of telling you that you look positively edible dressed like that."

"Not that I'm complaining, but you've seen me in jeans and a sweater before," I pointed out.

"Not with your hair pulled up and glistening lips that would tempt anyone to sample them," he said.

"It's just a messy bun," I practically purred as his lips moved to my ear, making goose bumps pop up on my arms.

"Trust me, it's hot as hell," he said.

"Well, I'm glad you like it, and thanks for getting me all hot and bothered now too with your assault on my mouth," I said as he stepped up behind me.

"Say it again," he whispered in my ear, wrapping his arms around my stomach to pull me flush against him.

"I'm glad you like it?" I asked, smiling at him through the mirror.

"What? No. Got you all hot and bothered," he clarified.

"You need an ego stroke?" I teased.

"It strokes something, sweetheart, just not my ego," he stated. "Which, at the moment, will have to be put on hold because I have plans for us."

"Am I dressed warm enough?"

"Yeah, it doesn't feel nearly as cold as it was yesterday. All the locals I talked with today claim this is the last warm day before winter sneaks in. I guess a cold front is moving in this evening, and after that, summer and even fall will be forgotten. I'm not entirely sure how they can be so adamant about it, but I guess if you've lived here all your life, you'd know the weather better than a couple Southerners. I figured we better seize the opportunity while we have it," he said, guiding me out the front door.

The sun was shining bright when we stepped outside. I relished the warmth of it, and after the bone-chilling rain from the previous evening, the heat felt heavenly. There was still a slight breeze, but it didn't cut through you like yesterday. These were the days we lived for back home, but they were few and far between. Humidity and heat indexes made up 80 percent of the climate in Florida.

"So what do you think?" he asked, indicating the rack with two mountain bikes strapped to the back of his Range Rover.

"We're going on a bike ride?" I whispered, slowly walking toward the mounted bicycles. I was confused how he had figured out another chink in my armor. It could just be a coincidence. No one here knew about the last bike ride I had ever taken. It was the one memory that belonged to me alone.

"I know you have that whole 'no exercise' thing going on, but I figured a leisurely bike ride wouldn't fall under that rule?" he asked, looking uncertain. "I just thought it would be funny after all the joking if we really did take a bike ride together," he added with a crooked grin.

"It's fine. It's just been a long time since I've ridden a bike," I said as memories of my last bike ride assaulted my senses. Pictures filled my head of my mom and me pedaling our pink-and-purple beach cruisers. She looked breathtakingly beautiful. It was a Sunday ritual for us to ride our bikes to the beach. We'd wheel them down the wooden steps to the sand below and ride along the water's edge while the wind blew through our hair. Afterward, we would stop at the ice-cream stand near the pier. We'd both get chocolate cones dipped in cherry hard shell. The memories were poignant, which was why I rarely visited them. Most of the time they were just too painful.

"Hey, you okay?" Nathan asked, dragging me away from my memories.

"Sure," I answered, pasting a smile on my face.

"When your smile doesn't quite reach your eyes, I know

you're just feeding me a line," he remarked, studying me intently.

"Really, it's nothing," I managed to say, although I was unsettled by his intensity and uncanny knack of being able to read me so well.

"I wish you would trust me," he muttered, opening the vehicle door for me.

"There's nothing to trust. I'm not hiding anything," I said, climbing in.

Nathan was still frowning as he climbed into the vehicle beside me.

"Are you expecting a jealous ex-boyfriend to suddenly show up and slash your tires?" I joked, trying to lighten the mood.

"Just put it this way: I wouldn't be surprised," he remarked, pulling his Range Rover onto the main road.

"Seriously, you need to relax and trust me when I say that some psycho will not be slashing your tires. So where are we going?"

"There's a mountain bike trail not far from here. According to Janice at the library, it's a relatively easy incline, but the view is amazing."

"Are you on a first-name basis with everyone in town?" I inquired. I had been in Woodfalls longer than Nathan, and even I didn't know as many people as he seemed to. Of course, he and I had known each other less than a week and we'd already been intimate, so what did that say about me? Only one word came to mind to describe Nathan: charming. He'd managed to charm the town much like he'd charmed me. His sexy radio voice didn't hurt, of course. It had a way of putting a person at ease.

"Pretty much," he answered as the last of the tension left him. "They all seem to think quite fondly of you."

"That's just because I'm new. I'm a novelty right now," I said. I shouldn't have been surprised. This was what a small town got you. It was what I said I wanted. "I'm sure they're already eyeing you to take my place as the new toy."

"I'm only interested in being your toy." He winked at me.

"That could end badly for you. I loved playing with my toys," I chirped before the full implication of my words had fully run through my head. "I meant to say you'd get sick of me playing with you so much," I added, burying myself further in innuendo hell.

"Honey, you can play with me as much as you want." He smirked.

"I bet." I blushed, making a point of not looking at his lap.

"It's pretty cute how you blush," he said, stroking a finger down my cheek.

"You seem to have that power over me," I admitted.

"Really? So, this is just for me?"

"Don't look so happy about it. I'm not thrilled that my feelings seem to be on display for you to see," I retorted.

"I like it. I'm not sure I remember the last time I was with a woman who allowed herself to be so open. It makes you unique, not to mention, it appeals to me in a very unexpected way," he reassured me, turning the vehicle down a road with a carved wooden sign that had the words *National Park* burned in it.

The road leading to the national park was composed of dirt and gravel and pocketed with multiple ruts. We bumped along for almost a mile before it opened up to a small parking lot where a rusted-out orange Ford truck and a small yellow VW Bug were parked. Large oak trees shaded the small parking lot with the last of their burnt orange–colored leaves. Judging by the amount of leaves that crunched underfoot as we unloaded the bikes, it wouldn't be long before the majestic trees were completely bare.

18. *A Day on the Trails*

NATHAN

Ashton was silent as I finished unloading the bikes, which had me second-guessing the whole trip. I knew once again she was keeping something from me, and yet I felt powerless on how to get her to open up. Maybe if we'd been dating for several months, I'd have the right to be more demanding, but the tentative relationship we had did not allow for that. My goal of charming her into my arms had worked according to plan, but what had been acceptable two days ago was no longer what I wanted. I knew I was scaling a precarious slope that could crash down on me at any moment. The smart thing would be to abide by the rules we had set and enjoy the moment. Unfortunately, I wasn't smart where she was concerned. I wanted more.

"You sure you're okay with this?" I asked, handing her one of the helmets.

"Only if you swear you won't laugh if I land on my ass, which seems likely since it always seems to happen when you're around."

"I solemnly swear I won't laugh if you fall on your ass," I proclaimed, raising my right hand for emphasis.

"Smart-ass," she complained, wheeling her bike toward the trail. "You go first until I get the hang of it," she added, straddling her bike.

"You'll be fine. Supposedly, you never forget how to ride a bike," I said, pedaling away. I rode for a hundred yards or so before venturing a look behind me to make sure she was okay. She looked like a natural, so obviously all her fears were for naught. It wasn't until I took in the clouded expression on her face that I guessed she wasn't enjoying the ride at all. Slowing to a stop, I straddled the bike, waiting for her to catch up.

"What's wrong?" she asked, looking somewhat distracted.

"Honey, I wanted to do something that you'd enjoy. I didn't mean for this to be some kind of torture chamber. Why don't we head back and we can do something else."

"No," she said in an unexpectedly stern manor. "I mean, I don't want to turn around. Really, I'm enjoying it."

"Sweets, you have a weird way of showing enjoyment. You look like you're in physical pain. Really, it won't be any skin off my nose if we head back."

"It's not that," she sighed heavily before looking up at me. I was shocked to see her in tears. "It's just, the last time I rode a bike, it was with my mom right before she died. We had this tradition where we would bike to the beach every week and ride along the shoreline. The last time we went, she was too exhausted to make it home, so my dad came to get us. A week later, she was too sick to ride at all, and three days after that, she went to the hospital and never came home—stage-four cancer. We never knew it. That last bike ride we took has always stuck with me. She was in a weird mood that day. In hindsight, I can't help wondering if at the time she suspected something was off," she answered as a lone tear streaked down her cheek.

"Oh, God, babe, I didn't realize," I said, using the pad of my thumb to wipe away her tear. "Let's go back. We'll do something else," I added, unprepared for the reaction her tears had on me. Usually, I viewed tears as a weapon that women readily used in their arsenal to keep men in line. Normally, I would have fled the scene at the first hint of tears, but Ashton's had the opposite effect on me.

"No, I don't want to leave," she insisted. "It's almost therapeutic. I've kept memories of her at bay for so long. It's nice."

"Right, so nice you're crying?" I asked skeptically.

"Bittersweet tears," she said, swiping the moisture off her cheeks and flashing me a tentative smile.

"And there's a difference?"

"A big difference, especially for me since I never cry the other kind," she admitted.

"Never?"

"Not since my mom died. I saw what a toll my tears had on my father and I vowed never to cry again."

I studied her for a moment, wishing I could figure her out. It amazed me the way she kept surprising me. When I had first been hired to find her, I'd studied the packet of pictures my client had sent me and saw nothing but a spoiled princess. At the time, I didn't care why she had run. I pretty much just assumed she'd skipped out to be with another man because I'd seen it so many times before. Every preconceived notion I had made before I found her was wrong. It was supposed to be me charming her, but somehow, she'd turned the tables and was the one charming me.

"So stop being a wuss and trying to weasel out of the bike ride," she said impishly, placing her feet on her pedals and taking off.

I took off after her, chuckling along the way. The tears were done now, which was a relief. Ashton continued to taunt and joke her way up the slow inclining trail. I allowed her to take the lead for purely selfish reasons since her ass looked incredible on a bike seat. By the time we reached the top, Ashton was breathing heavily and looked exhausted. I couldn't help ribbing her that if she exercised she'd have more stamina.

"My stamina was good enough last night," she answered.

Even though she gave as good as she got, I could tell she was more tired than she was willing to admit. At least the ride back down the trail was much easier.

"I blame the late-night canoe ride you took me on last night," she said, sinking into the passenger seat gratefully.

"You're probably right," I admitted, feeling guilty despite

my joking. I handed her the keys before I closed her door so she could warm up the Range Rover while I loaded the bikes.

The ride back to Ashton's was quiet. She rested her head back against the seat with her eyes shut practically the entire way. I smiled briefly at how whipped she looked. She wasn't lying when she said she was worn out.

"I have a few things to do this afternoon, but thought I'd come over later if that was okay with you?" I asked, finally breaking the silence as I pulled into her driveway.

"Sure," she answered, wearily pushing the vehicle door open.

"I'm thinking we'll stay in," I added, laughing as she staggered slightly. "You better take a nap. You look like you were dragged down the mountain."

"Your flattery is staggering. I could outride you any day," she bragged as she stifled another yawn.

I laughed again. "Go take a nap and I'll be back later with some dinner. Then we can discuss your bike-riding skills," I suggested, wagging my eyebrows at her.

"Great, now that we've gone on an actual bike ride, I can't tell if you mean 'bike ride,'" she said, pointing to the back of the vehicle, "or 'bike ride'"—moving her hips back and forth.

"We—" She shut the vehicle door before giving me the chance to confirm what she already knew.

I was still chuckling as I pulled out of her driveway, heading toward my motel room. Then the reality of the situation set in. It was obvious by the way that she opened up to me on the mountain that Ashton was starting to trust me. Two days ago I would've been happy about it, but now I couldn't help feeling like a fraud. I'd charmed my way into her bed on so many bogus pretenses that I no longer knew which ones were true and which were untrue. One startling fact that sat at the forefront of all my thoughts was that I no longer cared why she had run. I wasn't about to turn over her whereabouts to anyone. I also planned on telling her why I'd really come to Woodfalls. Not tonight, though. I wanted at least one more night with her before she made her choice. She'd most likely run once she knew, and I would let her go. I at least owed her that.

19. *Taking a Sick Day*

ASHTON

By the time I woke from my nap several hours later, I felt like I'd been hit by a truck or something. Every move I made was answered with an ache or pain in muscles I didn't even know I had. Sore muscles weren't my only issue either. My skin felt warm and dry like I had a sunburn. I actually felt pretty crummy. As icing on the cake, a headache also made itself known when I sat up to check the clock.

I was pretty sure I needed to get up and get ready since Nathan was coming over, but my body refused to cooperate. Anytime I felt sick like this I always panicked. I'd witnessed the symptoms firsthand with my mom. I watched them consume her until she was taken from me. Then I suffered from the same symptoms myself. Four years, three hundred fifty days ago. I was a different person then. Four years ago, I believed I could beat it. I accepted the news when they told me I would need a complete hysterectomy, even though I was only seventeen at the time. I pretended the hair loss didn't bother me as the chemo ravaged through my body, making me sicker than I could have ever imagined. I tolerated the looks of pity from my classmates and the snubs I received when I had to repeat my senior year since I missed half the year clutching the toilet, trying to rid my body of the toxins they were pumping into me. I accepted it all because I believed I could beat it. I had statistics on my side. We had caught it early. The doctors were confident that I wouldn't wind up like my mom, that we had an early diagnosis on our side, so I fought. I never gave up, and when I went into remission, I believed everything they had told me. I would be considered cured when I stayed in remission for five years. Time began a countdown as I kept the five-year mark in my head.

I finished my senior year of high school a loner, no longer the person I had been before I found out I had cancer. My so-called friends had graduated the year before and moved on with their own lives, all glad they no longer had to face me. The rest of the students avoided me like the plague, like they were afraid they would catch what I had. High school became nothing more than torture as I avoided school functions. I just couldn't take the looks of pity. I would have avoided prom completely if my father hadn't bullied Shawn's father into making Shawn take me. Giving Shawn my virginity that night was my rebellious way of trying to finally feel normal, not that it worked.

With high school finally behind me, I immersed myself in college, hoping to make up for lost time. Fighting cancer made me realize how fragile life was, and I was anxious to start feeling alive. The moment happened the day they handed me my diploma. I was two hundred days shy of reaching the five-year mark, and I was confident I would make it. Ten days later, my body began to ache and I became fatigued. I didn't need a doctor to tell me the cancer had returned. I recognized the symptoms. I had been there before. That was the day I wrote my bucket list and began to make the necessary arrangements to leave. One thing I knew without a shadow of a doubt was that I couldn't put my father through another cancer crisis. He had watched my mother die and then had to watch me battle it seven years later. I would never forget the pain in his eyes as he worried himself sick that my fate would be the same as hers. He wept when the doctors told him I was in remission, confessing that he'd been so afraid he'd lose me also. I could not face telling him I was sick again. I knew it would destroy him, just like I knew I no longer had the will to fight it. The cancer would not be happy until it took me. So I left.

My father received a letter from me filled with lies once I was gone. I claimed I was sick of his hovering, that I was done being treated like a child, and I needed time to discover the person I was supposed to be, without his meddling. I told him he was suffocating me, and I could no longer live in the same town with him. I knew my words would hurt him, but that was my intent. I wanted him to hate me, to think I was ungrateful so he could move on. Hate was easier to overcome than grief.

I shivered slightly in my bed, probably from a fever, but also from the memories. I missed my father. I missed his words of wisdom, his goofy laugh, and the way he loved to drag me to see old sci-fi movies. He was serious at times and needy other times, but terrific the rest of the time. It broke my heart that I would never see him again.

I was still lying in bed when Nathan arrived half an hour later with pizza and a bottle of wine in hand.

"You're sick," he said, taking one look at me as I pulled the front door open to let him in.

"Probably from the outside shower we took last night," I joked.

"Crap. I'm sorry, honey," he said, setting the pizza and wine on my coffee table.

"I'm just sorry I'm messing up our date. We don't seem to have the best of luck with our dates. Between me passing out, your allergic reaction, a canoe ride in driving rain, and now my annoying cold, I'm beginning to think someone is trying to tell us something," I contemplated, sitting on my couch.

"They're just trying to test our resilience," he said, tucking a quilt around me from the rack that hung on the wall.

I snorted. "I don't know. I think maybe we're a part of some cosmic joke. Someone is getting a laugh at our expense."

He threw his head back and laughed at my words.

"What?" I asked.

"I kid you not. I had the same fucking thought last night when the sky opened up on us. I don't care, though. The cosmic gods can throw as many curveballs as they want at us."

"You're awfully cocky tempting fate like that," I said, trying to keep my voice light, even though the idea scared the shit out of me. I knew the ultimate move fate could use, and the outcome would change us both forever.

"I just believe in making my own fate. Life may be a greedy bastard at times, but I'm confident I can handle whatever is thrown my way," he said, grabbing plates and wineglasses from the lone cabinet in my kitchen.

"I didn't have you tagged as an optimist. I would have pegged you for a pessimist for sure," I said.

"Shit, I'm one hundred percent pessimist, but that doesn't mean I don't believe I make my own fate. Let me guess, you're one hundred percent optimistic," he commented, handing me a piece of pizza.

"I used to be. I'm not all that sure I am anymore," I mused, nibbling at my pizza, although I wasn't all that hungry. "I've changed a lot lately. I guess you could call it growing up. Maybe I'm becoming boring and dull in my old age."

"Interesting," he pondered, taking a big bite from his own pizza. "Boring? You're far from boring. You may be stoic, but there's nothing dull about you."

"In what way?" I asked, unnerved that he considered me stoic. To the best of my knowledge, stoic meant someone who endures without complaint. It bothered me a little that he saw me that way despite the lies I had fed him. *Stoic* wouldn't be the word I would use to describe myself. *Liar* was more accurate, but of course, he wouldn't know that about me. I'd always been a truthful person. Really, all the half-truths and lies had turned me into someone I hardly recognized anymore. I'd convinced myself that was my intention all along. After living so long under a microscope with everyone knowing my every secret, the lies I told now were intended to shield me.

"Maybe it's because you're always so upbeat, although every once in a while you get this little hint of sadness in your eyes. Sometimes, it's like you're hiding something or a part of yourself. You quickly distill it, but I've seen it," he answered, grabbing another slice of pizza.

I waited him for him to go for broke and ask what I was hiding. His intuitiveness was dead-on, and I couldn't help wondering if it was the reporter in him or just a gift he had. I prepared myself mentally for how I would handle this question, knowing that he of all people could not know the truth. I never wanted him to look at me with pity, or worse yet, run for the hills the moment the big C was mentioned.

The conversation kind of fizzled after that as I continued to nibble on my slice of pizza while he devoured half the pie.

"Not hungry?" he asked as I set my half-eaten piece of pizza on the coffee table.

"Not really," I answered, settling back against the cushions of the couch. "I know I'm being a downer. You don't have to stay and keep me company," I added reluctantly.

"Do you want me to leave?" he asked inquisitively.

"No, but I know it can't be much fun hanging out with a sickie. Besides, aren't we supposed to be tired of each other? I'm new to this whole relationship thing, but aren't you supposed to be giving some speech about how you need your space and that I'm cramping your style with my clingy ways?"

"First of all, is it wrong that the sickie thing is turning me on? Secondly, I've discovered there's nothing ordinary about our relationship. I enjoy being with you and there's nowhere else I'd rather be. Plus, I'm not sure you could be clingy even if you tried," he answered, gathering our leftover dinner and plates and depositing them in my kitchen. "Would you like more wine or some water?" he asked, coming back to get my half-empty wineglass.

"Water would be great, but you don't have to wait on me," I said, starting to rise only to have him gently shove me back to the couch.

"Getting you a glass of water won't kill me. Why don't you find something for us to watch," he said, handing me the remote.

"You sure you want me to be in charge of the remote?" I asked, switching on the television. "That means you'll be stuck watching my new favorite chick show that's filled to the brim with estrogen."

"And what show would be?" he quizzed, handing me my glass of water before settling on the couch beside me.

"I've been on a *Sex and the City* rerun kick now that it's on demand," I admitted. "It's jam-packed with helpful information on the opposite sex," I added flirtatiously, though I kept out the fact that it was *Sex and the City* that had given me the idea to pick up a stranger in a bar. Of course, the bar scene in New York, where the show took place, was a far cry from Woodfalls.

"I've seen them all. They're not all that bad, though Samantha is a major slut and pretty obnoxious. I've always liked the brunette the most," he said, snaking an arm around me and pulling me in the crook of his arm. "I forget what her name is, though."

"Charlotte," I answered for him.

"That's it, Charlotte," he clarified.

"So, you're telling me you've watched every episode? What about the movies?"

"Those too. Television is my guilty pleasure. My job requires a lot of travel, so I stream a lot of episodes on my iPad."

"What else do you watch?" I asked, switching to the on-demand channel.

"You name it, I've probably seen it. Especially if it's on cable. Those are edgier and they show boobies and stuff. There's one on HBO that's absolutely brilliant about a news channel. There's a few on Bravo and a few other channels I like."

"As long as they have boobies, right?" I teased.

"Heck yeah," he laughed.

"CW shows?" I inquired.

"Sadly, no. I think I'm just too old to relate to teenage shows about vampires or werewolves," he said, shuddering distastefully. "What about you?"

"I'm a bit of a novice. I didn't watch a whole lot of television in college, and I was too preoccupied in high school. I'm kind of just now discovering what I like. I find I'm a bit obsessive when I find a show I enjoy. I'll stay up late watching five or six episodes until I've seen the whole series," I admitted, starting a *Sex and the City* episode where I had left off.

"That sounds like me too," he said, pulling me snugly in his arms before reaching over to switch off the light on the end table.

We were only halfway through the first episode when I fell asleep, cocooned in his arms.

I woke up the next morning in my bed, feeling disoriented. I had no recollection of how I had gotten here, let alone stripping off my clothes. The other side of the bed was empty, but the head imprint in the pillow made it clear I had not slept alone.

"How you doing?" Nathan asked, breaking through my thoughts as he entered my room with a bottle of Advil and a tall glass of water.

"Not bad," I said.

"Liar," he mocked, reaching over to feel my forehead. "You were pretty warm when I woke up a couple hours ago."

"Did you leave?" I asked, taking in his jeans and flannel shirt, which were different than what he had on the previous day.

"Yeah, the cold front everyone was buzzing about yesterday definitely moved in. They're now saying we may get up to a foot of snow."

"Really? It's not even October," I exclaimed. Forgetting I was clad in only my bra and panties, I sat up and just caught the blanket as it slid down, exposing my lace bra. His eyes rested on it for a second before returning to my face. I flushed. My confidence from the other night was long gone, and I was unsure what the proper behavior was for what was going on between us.

"Here," he said, handing me a couple of pills.

"Thanks," I said, still clutching the blanket to my chest.

"You're going to have to release your death grip on the blanket to take a drink," he chuckled.

"Nuh-uh," I mumbled, popping the pills in my mouth before reaching for my glass of water with my now free hand.

"You don't have to be shy with me," he said, lifting my chin with his fingers so our eyes met.

"This part is new to me," I confessed.

"It is for me too, but I'm not going to lie, I like seeing you all sleep-rumpled in the morning," he admitted.

"Really?" I asked as a warm feeling that had nothing to do with my fever spread through me. I knew I shouldn't be happy. I should be keeping him at arm's length, but the idea that he wanted to stay made me feel warm and fuzzy inside.

"Really," he answered, leaning in to rub his lips against my cheek. "Hmm, you feel warmer than earlier," he observed, placing his palm against my forehead.

"It's just a cold. I guess that picnic in the rain you planned the other night wasn't the best idea," I said, pulling back slightly to dislodge his hand. I didn't want to make a big deal over my fever.

"Maybe I should take you to the doctor."

"It's just a fever. People get them all the time," I argued, tamping back my panic. I most definitely did not want to go to the doctor.

"I guess you have a point," he said, gently pushing me back against my pillows. "You should at least rest," he said, tucking my blankets around me.

"I should call Fran," I protested, reaching for my phone.

"I kind of already told her," he said, looking sheepish.

"What? When?" I asked.

"I stopped off at her store to stock up on some supplies in case it really does snow. I told her you felt feverish and she told me to tell you to stay home. She seemed quite worried about you. She told me if it snows like they think, that you're to take tomorrow off too, and that it was an order, so no arguing."

"She acts tough, but she's nothing but a softie," I said, trying to sound blasé. I could imagine why she was worried. Fran was the only person I had confided in. I knew my secret was safe with her, though I knew my refusal to see a doctor worried her. I felt bad about the stress I was adding on her already frail shoulders, but not enough to have my fears confirmed. I didn't want hospitals with their endless tests, poking, and poisonous toxins. I wanted to do things on my terms this time. It was my decision, and I planned to stick with it even though some doubt had begun to creep in. I was pretty convinced the man beside me had something to do with that.

"I like her. Her crusty attitude is highly entertaining."

"Yeah, I like her too, a lot," I agreed. "I forgot to ask you yesterday if you were able to retrieve everything."

"With the help of some locals. Needless to say, I owe a handful of guys a round at Joe's. Turns out, it was more of a pain in the ass than I thought it would be," he admitted. "Not to mention, I may have been called a pansy when they saw the lanterns and candle remnants."

"I bet. Some of those guys are pretty gruff and set in their ways. It's best to just ignore them," I said, stifling a yawn.

"Oh, I didn't ignore them. I told them at least I got the girl," he said, chuckling as he pulled the drapes closed.

"That'll show 'em," I said, closing my eyes. "Thanks for checking in on me and telling Fran I'd be out today," I added, fighting my drowsiness. I figured he'd be ready to leave now that he had checked on me.

My assumptions were wrong, though. I drifted in and out of a fever-induced sleep the majority of the day, and he was always there when I woke. I knew I should send him away. We were breaking every rule I had set, and would only be making things harder for ourselves in the end, but I couldn't find the will to send him away. His presence was oddly comforting as he pushed more Advil and water on me whenever I woke up. By the time the sun was setting, my fever had broken and I was ready to eat the hearty stew he had cooked for me in my kitchen.

"A man who cooks is a rare treasure," I observed, balancing my bowl on my lap as I dunked a hunk of French bread in the thick broth. I was perched on my couch, bundled up in the same quilt from the night before, glad to finally be out of my bed. My relief that my fever had passed was tangible. I wasn't ready for my symptoms to be known.

"Is that the only thing that makes me a treasure?" he said, sitting down and lifting my feet onto his lap.

"Hmmm, I'll have to get back to you on that," I answered,

lost in his touch. Who knew getting your feet massaged could be so sensual? It seemed the more time I spent with Nathan, the more items I realized had been sorely missing from my list. Even something as simple as having him cook for me had made my chest ache from the sweetness of it. I'd been so focused on experiencing things like jumping off bridges and getting drunk that actual human contact activities had never occurred to me. I was so bent on keeping everyone at arm's length that somewhere along the way I'd shut myself completely off from the things that should have mattered. The fact that I'd actually taken Fran's and Tressa's advice was a relief. Of course, I knew a big majority of the sensations and feelings I was experiencing had a lot to do with the person I was sharing them with.

"Do you like that?" he asked when I sighed with pleasure as his fingers kneaded the ball of my foot.

"It's fair," I answered, giggling when he tickled the bottom of it.

"Fair?" he growled, pulling on my foot.

I set my empty bowl on the table. "You can't be good at everything. However will we fit your head out the front door?" I laughed.

"I'm far from perfect," he said quietly.

"Nobody's perfect," I clarified.

"Not even you?"

"Ha, I'm far from perfect," I snorted.

"Why do you say that? From everything I've heard from Fran and your best friends, you practically float on a gold cloud playing a harp. I quote, 'She's the nicest person you'll ever meet and if you hurt her I'll cut off your balls.'"

"Let me guess: Fran?"

"Would you believe she and Tressa pretty much gave me the same speech?"

"I'm touched they think so highly of me, but they really haven't known me that long. I have an uncanny habit of disappointing most people I know," I admitted. I instantly regretted my words. I knew it sounded like I was painting a woe-is-me picture of myself, and that was the last thing I wanted.

"Shit, that had an after-school special ring to it," I joked, trying to make light of the moment.

"Maybe you just don't see yourself clearly, or maybe you've set the bar so high for yourself that when you don't quite make the mark you think you've failed."

"Maybe," I agreed, though I knew he was wrong. If he knew the facts, he'd know just how wrong he was, but then that was the point. He'd never know the facts, so there was no reason I should obsess over it.

"Okay, so now that we've established we're not perfect, whatever will we do with our tarnished selves?" he asked, trailing his hand up over my calf. "Maybe we should work on perfecting this," he added, trailing his hand farther up my leg.

"True, practice makes perfect, doesn't it?" I agreed as he hauled me into his lap.

"And God knows we definitely want perfection on this," he said, dropping his lips on mine. Any other talking was forgotten as I lost myself in the touch of his lips as they discovered parts of my body they had missed the first night we spent together. No longer needing the quilt, I pushed it off me so he could have easier access to the places I wanted his lips the most.

"I think you must like that," he said when his tongue made my sensitive nipple hard.

I nodded, pulling his head back to me.

"And this?" he asked, trailing his lips down my stomach. My only answer came out as more of a pant as he shimmied my pants down over my hips. Desire roared through me like a runaway train as his mouth continued to move down before settling between my legs.

20. *The First Snow*

NATHAN

I was fucked and I knew it. The moment I touched Ashton, I realized that getting her out of my system was easier said than done. In my stupidity, I'd convinced myself that once I had her it would curb the desire that crackled like a live wire between us. What an idiot. After lying with her curled up in my arms for the third night in a row, losing myself in her body yet again, it had become glaringly obvious that getting her out of my system was like trying to get off crack. It was an ironic analogy, but she was my drug of choice. Everything about her pulled me in and clouded my mind more sufficiently than any drug would ever be able to. When I was with her I was no longer the same person. Laughter in my regular life was sporadic at best, and yet, with Ashton it was as natural as breathing. Each new discovery I made about her was as enchanting as the last and made me want to continue probing until I knew everything that made her tick. It was becoming almost painful not to know the secrets she hid behind her smiles and jokes. I needed to know what we were facing. The complexity of our relationship was daunting. A week ago I would have balked at it, but everything was different now. In a week she had changed me completely.

I tightened my arm around her taut midriff, pulling her more snugly into my arms. She sighed with satisfaction in her sleep, and though I had just made love to her a short time ago, I immediately became aroused just watching her. Every curve. Every lightly colored bit of peach fuzz on her stomach. I buried my face in her hair, inhaling her, feeling drunk from the scent. I felt comfortable lying here. So much so that I drifted to sleep, wrapped around the woman I wasn't supposed to fall for.

I woke the next morning to Ashton's excited squeals. I sat up blurry eyed and smiled when I saw her literally dancing at the front window. "Did you win a new car or something?" I teased, climbing out of bed to stand behind her.

"It's snowing," she crowed, clapping her hands with glee.

"I'm taking it you feel better?" I asked, chuckling at her enthusiasm.

"Much. We have to go out and play in the snow," she said, frantically pulling warm clothes out of her wardrobe.

"I don't think it's going anywhere, sweets," I said, placing my hands on her to still her frantic movements.

"Oh, you're naked," she said, stating the obvious as her eyes darted down to my morning companion.

"Yeah, we sort of went to bed that way," I teased, watching as a delicate shade of pink crept up her neck, staining her cheeks. "Does it make you uncomfortable?" I asked.

"What? No, it's just like, you know, 'Ta-da. Here I am.' It threw me off," she stumbled out.

"Well, for your information, this is pretty common for most guys in the morning."

"Really? How unfortunate," she said.

"Get dressed," I laughed. "The snow is calling your name."

"Snow?" she said, looking momentarily confused. "Right, snow," she said finally, making me laugh again as she hurried off to the bathroom with an armload of clothes.

Fifteen minutes later, we were out in front of her cottage watching big snowflakes fall lazily from the sky. The ground was already covered with an inch of snow, making crunching sounds beneath our feet. Everything was peaceful and serene.

"It's beautiful," Ashton exclaimed in a hushed tone as big flakes landed on her upturned face. She slowly turned in a circle with her arms outstretched.

"I'm sure by December you'll feel different," I observed.

"I won't be here in December to . . ." She trailed off.

"Really? I was under the impression you planned on living here permanently," I said, watching her bite her lip. From her expression, I could tell she had slipped up.

"Oh, I haven't decided," she answered. "Do you think enough will fall to make a snow angel and a snowman?" she asked, changing the subject.

I studied her for a moment, debating whether I should

pursue the issue. The forced gaiety in her voice convinced me to let it drop. "At the rate it's falling, I bet by noon you'll be able to make a decent snow angel at least. Do you want to go for a walk?" I asked, offering her my hand.

"Yes," she answered as some of her excitement from earlier returned.

"Are you warm enough?" I asked before we headed off toward the trail behind her house.

"Yeah, I can barely walk from all the layers you forced on me," she reminded me.

"Trust me, you'll be thankful for all those layers," I said, linking my gloved fingers with hers. "Besides, just yesterday you were laid up with a fever and a cold. You probably shouldn't even be outside."

"I'm fine. There's no way I'm missing the first snow."

"You're awfully stubborn."

"So? You're bossy, and I overlook that," she reminded me.

"Not bossy. I just like things to get done the way I want and direct others to follow them out," I said, defending myself.

"Yeah, that doesn't sound bossy," she teased, rolling her eyes. "Have you always 'not bossed' people around?" she added.

"Liked things my way? Probably. When I was younger and it was just my mom and me, I felt the pressure of being the man of the house. My mom always seemed to have the weight of the world on her shoulders, so I wanted to help relieve some of the pressure for her. By the time I was thirteen, I'd taken over all the maintenance of the trailer we lived in. I became an expert at fixing leaky faucets, reattaching loose paneling, and making sure our roof didn't leak during rainy season. Home Depot became my playground on weekends, as I took every workshop they offered. Seeing my interests, I think my mom had the idea that I would grow up to be an architect or a contractor. I think she was disappointed when I told her I wanted to be a journalist."

"Why would she be disappointed?"

"I think she was under the impression that a journalist was a fluff job that I wouldn't make any money doing. She wanted me to have security and money for a rainy day. Years of living week to week had jaded her and she put little stock into dreams. She eventually got over her aversion to my job choice but didn't live long enough to see it amount to anything."

"I'm sorry. I bet she'd be proud of your successes if she saw you now," Ashton said earnestly.

"I'm not entirely sure she would. I think she'd be disappointed in some of the decisions I've made."

"I think everyone feels that way."

"Do you?" I asked, keeping my voice casual.

"Of course, but we can't please everyone. All we can hope is that we learn from the decisions we've made and anyone we've hurt along the way will forgive us someday."

"So, you believe that if someone betrays you, they deserve a second chance?" I asked.

"I would hope I'd get a second chance, so yes, I'd give someone another chance," she said with an intensity that matched my own.

"Fair enough," I said, getting the answer I was hoping for.

I didn't know if that applied to me, but I had to hope so. I kept delaying telling her the truth, but I knew the clock was ticking, and I would have to tell her soon.

"Besides being a handyman, what else were you like when you were younger?" she asked as we trampled through the snow.

"Aren't you bored hearing me talk?" I inquired.

"No way. I like hearing your stories. Plus, I'm not going to lie—you could read the dictionary and your sexy-as-sin voice would make it appealing."

"I've heard women say that about my voice before. What about it makes it so appealing, so I can home in on it?" I teased.

"Believe me, you don't have to try any harder. If it got any sexier, you'd leave women in puddles wherever you went."

"Are you telling me it liquefies you?" I asked, pulling her into my arms. "So, if I talk lower like this, does it make you damp in all the right areas?" I persisted, dropping my voice to just above a whisper.

"Just being with you does that," she admitted, biting her lip in the way that hit me in the right spot. "Of course, I'm sure I'm not supposed to admit that."

"Sweetheart, the fact that you're so open with how you're feeling is one of the things I like the most about you. Your blush gives away some of it," I said, rubbing my gloved thumb over her cheek. "But I love how you don't try to hide it like most women."

"You mean you love that I have the dating skills of a baboon?" she mocked. "Me monkey, I like you, can I climb you?" she added, laughing halfway through her speech.

"God, only you could make that sound hot," I said, hauling her into my arms. "And just so you know, you can climb me anytime you want," I added, dropping my mouth to iced lips. She parted her lips at my insistence, clinging to me as I deepened the kiss. I placed my hands on her hips, dragging her lower half to my body so I could emphasize just what her words did to me.

"Damn your layers," she complained, pulling back with aggravation.

I bit back my own groan as my body strained toward hers. "We could go back to the house," I suggested. "I could get a fire started in the fireplace," I enticed, capturing her lips again with mine.

"Deal," she agreed.

21. *The Snow Angel*

ASHTON

The snow outside provided the perfect excuse to lie around all day being lazy. We pretty much did nothing but watch TV until dark. The flames from the fireplace made the shadows dance on the walls. For once, it wasn't me who fell asleep first. Nathan slept next to me on the thick pallet of blankets we had laid out in front of the fireplace where we had just made love. At this point, to deny that it was just sex would cheapen what we had shared. My skin still felt the tingle of his touch while my mind replayed how he had looked in the firelight as he slid into me. Unlike the other two times, when all our focus centered on reaching the wave of ecstasy, this time we took the time to discover and enjoy each other's bodies. It was slow and delicious. I curiously explored his body, discovering what he liked. He groaned when my hand had closed around him, stroking him. He allowed my touch for a few moments before rolling on top of me and taking me. His pace was slow and sure as he brought me to the edge countless times, retreating each time just before I went over. Each time I was close, he would drop his mouth to mine, swallowing my gasps and pleas for release. Eventually, his own willpower had faded away and he took us both over the edge at the same time.

In all the ecstasy and pleasure, my emotions had now become more clouded than I cared to handle. My feelings for him were beginning to eclipse the plans I had set. I didn't want to be one of those women who confused lust with love. I barely knew him, so it couldn't be love. Besides, I'd always told myself I didn't believe in insta-love. I'd seen that in college when I watched my fellow students fall into one another's arms, professing their love after only a couple of dates and then breaking up a few weeks later. It always seemed like it was the girl who took it the hardest, while the guys would move on like nothing happened. I was not that kind of girl, and yet, I couldn't deny that I didn't feel something for Nathan. I wanted to be with him, to confide in him. I wanted to tear up our imaginary no-attachments contract. But most of all, I didn't want to leave him.

I quietly moved out from under Nathan's arms. The direction my thoughts had taken now had me completely annoyed. My clothes lay in a heap on the floor where we had left them in our anxiousness to get naked. I threw them on along with my heavy parka and knitted hat and headed outside to clear my head.

The white scene that greeted me was just as beautiful under the moonlight. Thanks to the unseasonably cold weather, a good six inches of snow blanketed the ground, and the tree branches above my head were all covered with fresh powder. I grinned with delight as I hopped off the small front porch. I walked out several feet into an open space and threw myself backward, letting the cottonlike snow cushion my fall. I fanned my arms out around me, creating my first-ever snow angel. The moment felt bittersweet. Just a few days ago I'd been worried that I wouldn't be able to finish all the items on my list, but now thanks to Nathan, I was less than seven items from finishing. Tears filled my eyes. The number seemed so final, and for a moment, I wished I had set the number higher. I knew I was being ridiculous. It wasn't as if the list held power over when my life would end, but at the moment, it felt like it.

"A penny for your thoughts," Nathan said, approaching from behind. His words seemed to burst my inner dam. Tears I never let myself shed flowed hot and fast down my cheeks as he lay down on the ground beside me.

"Hey, what is this?" Nathan asked, sitting up and pulling me onto his lap. "I'm sorry, sweetheart. I didn't mean to wake up and bother you." I knew he was teasing, of course. I tried to answer him, to tell him I was just being stupid, but the tears made talking impossible. Everything I'd been bottling up for the last four months flowed out of me in a torrent. I had to give Nathan credit. He didn't run for the hills like most males would have when faced with an inconsolable sobbing mess. Instead, he rocked me in his arms, rubbing my back. Eventually, the tears slowed and the cold and dampness from the snow began to seep through our clothes. I stood up, keeping my eyes averted from his, knowing he'd want answers. And I was ready to tell him. He deserved the truth, but before I did I wanted one more night in his arms when he didn't look at me with contempt for my cowardice or, worse yet, with pity.

Neither of us talked as we entered the cottage. Nathan stripped my damp clothes from my body so the fire could warm my skin. After removing his own clothes, he swept me up in his arms and carried me to bed, where he climbed in next to me. Wrapping his arms around me, he rolled onto his back, dragging me with him so I was lying on top of him with my body flush against his. Desperate to forget everything that stood between us, I tangled my hands in his hair and ground my mouth on his. The intensity of my feelings roared through me as I hungrily searched and found his tongue with my own. Maybe he sensed my need, or his own desire equaled mine, but he tangled his own hands in my hair, pulling me even closer. Our lips smashed together with bruising intensity as we both fed our hunger. My movements on his body matched our kiss as I moved against him, fueling the fire between us to a frenzied high. Wanting more, I broke the kiss and ran my lips down his jaw, nipping his scruff-covered chin before trailing down his neck and over his pecs. His hands once again grabbed my hair, but I completely took control. I felt possessed, forcing both of his arms above his head. My mouth continued to travel down his body and still it wasn't enough. He groaned, trying again to use his hands on me, but I forced them back once more. I continued even lower with my mouth, finding the destination I knew we both wanted. I showered the same amount of attention on him as he had earlier on me. I couldn't help feeling satisfied as he moaned my name. I allowed him to pull me back up to straddle his body, but that was all the control I would give him. This was my turn. I guided him inside me, rocking backward until he filled me completely. I was in charge of controlling the pace, and I marveled at the power I held just by moving my hips one way or another. Move fast and his eyes would glaze over with desire, never leaving my face. Move slower and I got to feel him hold himself rigid inside me as I moved. Enjoying my power, I tormented him with my movements, placing my mouth back down to his. His tongue entered as I placed my hands on his chest. I set a new pace that matched the movements of his tongue. Close to the edge, I pushed my pelvis down against him until he was buried in me deeper than he'd ever been. My movement sent us both over the edge and he shouted my name as he pulled me down hard against him one last time.

I collapsed on his chest, breathing heavily. All the energy I'd felt just moments ago had drifted away like a kite on a windy day. "Sorry," I said, trying to catch my breath.

"For what? Oh my God," he replied, running his hand over my bare back.

"So, you liked it?" I asked.

" 'Like' isn't even close to the right word," he replied. "Hey, not to change the subject after something as unbelievable as that, but do you want to talk about what happened outside?" he asked, continuing to rub my back.

"Not tonight. Is that okay?" I asked, rising up on my elbow so I could look at him.

"Are you okay now?" he inquired.

I took a moment to take stock of his question. Was I all right? Oddly, I felt much better. I knew using sex as a Band-Aid wouldn't lessen the truth, but at the moment, I allowed myself to shove my problems in a drawer. A drawer that could wait at least another day to be evaluated.

"Yeah, I'm okay," I finally answered, lying back on top of him. He continued to stroke my back as my eyelids became heavy. "I wish we could sleep this way," I murmured as he shifted me off him.

"Let me clean up, and your wish is my command," he said, rising from the bed.

By the time he returned, I was more asleep than awake as he pulled me into his arms and rested my head on his chest.

"I can feel your heart," I mumbled as my eyes closed.

His reply came from far away. I must have imagined it because as sleep pulled me under completely, it sounded like he said, "It is your heart now."

Nathan was gone from the bed when I woke the next morning. I could hear him talking in a hushed tone as I stretched before climbing out of bed. Grabbing my robe off the back of my bedroom door, I headed out to see what he was up to. I found him standing in front of the fireplace with his back to me. The hand that wasn't holding the phone gripped the mantel with an intensity that surprised me. I caught the tail end of his conversation as I paused in the doorway.

"Tomorrow is soon enough. I need to prepare things," he said in a hard tone I'd never heard him use before. "No, tomorrow," he repeated before ending the call.

"Everything okay?" I asked, sliding my arms around his waist and resting my face against his back.

"It's fine," he answered, setting his phone on the mantel and placing his hands on top of mine. "My boss is just being persistent."

"I thought you took a few weeks off."

"I did, but it looks like that won't be panning out."

"Are you leaving?" My voice cracked.

"Not right away," he said, turning around to wrap his arms around me. "What would you like to do today?" he asked, changing the subject.

"Would you be up for a double date? Tressa has been texting me all week, begging us to join her and the guy she likes for an indie concert by her campus. It means you'll be stuck hanging out with a CW crowd," I teased.

"She wants us to tag along on her date?" he asked skeptically.

"Not 'tag along.' Double date. I think she's dealing with nerves. She's been with Jackson so long that she's nervous seeing someone else. Do you mind?"

"For you, anything," he answered, dropping a quick peck on my lips. "I need to head to my hotel for a few hours, but I'll pick you up later. That way maybe we can see a movie while we're in the city."

"Sounds good. I'll text her and get the deets," I said, plucking up my own cell phone from the coffee table. "Will you be able to get the Range Rover out?" I added.

"I should, it's a sport-utility vehicle with four-wheel drive. I'll be back in a few hours," he said, placing his lips tenderly on mine.

"Hurry," I said, already missing him even though he wasn't gone yet.

"I'll be back before you know it," he said with the same reluctance I was feeling.

He closed the door quietly behind him and I felt bereft standing in my living room by myself. After being practically inseparable for the last five days, it felt strange to be alone. Irrational thoughts, sure, but I shook them off and headed to my bathroom so I could get ready.

22. *Phase Two*

NATHAN

I was still thinking about the phone call earlier with my client when I arrived at my hotel after leaving Ashton. Everything about the conversation had set my teeth on edge and made me want to put my fist through something, preferably the face of the fuck who hired me. I paced in my room trying to calm myself and work through my plan, which seemed to be spiraling out of control. I still stood by my decision to call the client and disclose Ashton's whereabouts, but I wanted us to be prepared. The time for secrets was long gone. By the end of the night, Ashton would know the real reason I was here. My only hope was that I could show her that my feelings for her had changed and that I would never let anyone hurt her ever again. I knew my plan was shaky. Ashton could hate me for my betrayal and take off without ever looking back, but it was the only feasible option.

I had stayed awake most of the night debating how I wanted to handle the situation before finally coming to this conclusion. I toyed with the idea of never reporting back to my client and leaving him with nothing. That wouldn't solve anything for Ashton, though. If he wanted her back bad enough, he'd just hire someone else to find her. Ashton would spend her life running away, never trusting anyone unless I put a stop to it. If this worked, her life of running could be put to a rest once and for all. Tomorrow morning we would face her demon and send him back to the hole he belonged in. My reputation in my field would be trashed, but I didn't give a damn. It had been a long time since I enjoyed my job anyway. Hell, I wasn't sure if I had ever enjoyed it.

Phase two of my plan could equally backfire in my face, but it was a risk I was willing to take. My surprise for Ashton today, though underhanded, would hopefully serve as something that would tie her down. Something that would form an attachment with her, which she worked so hard to keep at bay.

Glancing at the clock on the nightstand, I realized I was already fifteen minutes late for my appointment. I hurried out of my room with the box of supplies I'd bought from Fran the day before. Tossing the box on the backseat, I threw the vehicle in gear and headed toward my destination. I smiled for the first time since leaving Ashton earlier as I pulled into the dirt parking lot. Phase two of making Ashton mine was waiting for me just beyond the door in front of me.

23. *Wilma*

ASHTON

Two hours later, I was ready and sitting on my couch watching another episode of my show when Nathan knocked on the door once before entering. Relieved he was back, I jumped to my feet as he strode across the room and gathered me in his arms.

"Woman, what kind of spell have you cast over me that I don't like to be away from you for even a few hours?" he said, showering kisses over my exposed neck.

"Well, I may have slipped you a love potion," I said without thinking. I instantly regretted my words, wishing I could recall them. Mentioning "love," no matter how innocent, went completely against the rules we had set.

He stiffened for a moment, and I wished I could've bitten off my tongue. "It must be working because I feel completely intoxicated when I'm with you," he finally said, cupping my face in his hands and placing a kiss on each corner of my mouth before going all in. Thank God he didn't take my words seriously.

"By the way, you look amazing," he said, breaking the kiss. "Did you wear your hair up again to drive me nuts?" he asked, fingering a tendril that had escaped the elaborate twist I had gathered my hair in.

"Why, is it working?" I asked with false innocence.

"If you consider the inner battle I'm struggling with: whether I should take you out and let other guys gawk at you, or whether I should drag you to bed and show you just what your pinned-up hair does to me," he growled, pulling me close.

"I thought guys liked girls to wear their hair down?"

"Not with a delectable neck like yours. Your neck begs to be kissed. It's as appetizing as any banquet and twice as appealing," he murmured. "Now, stop distracting me, I have a surprise for you," he added, suddenly looking jittery.

"A surprise?"

"I left it in the car. You wait here," he said, still looking slightly off.

Puzzled at what the surprise could be, I waited in the center of the room for him to return.

"Okay, sit on the couch and close your eyes," he said, cracking the front door open a fraction to give me the instructions.

I settled on my couch, mystified, with my eyes closed. I heard him push the door open and then shut.

"Okay, open your eyes," he said just as I heard a little meowing noise.

"Oh my," I gasped, taking in the little fluff ball in his hands. "You got me a kitten?" I asked quietly.

"If you don't want her, I'll keep her," Nathan said, sitting across from me with the small orange kitten cradled in his hands.

"I've always wanted a cat, but the time never seemed right," I said, stroking a finger down the soft fur of her neck.

"Right now sounds like a good time to me," he said, handing her over.

"Oh my," I repeated. "She's so tiny and fluffy."

"She's the runt of the litter and the last one to be claimed."

"I know nothing about cats," I objected, knowing it wouldn't be fair to take her when my future was so uncertain, and yet I wanted her with a sudden passion that shocked me. Maybe it was her soft purring or the way she snuggled in my lap, but she already felt like mine.

"That's the wonderful thing about Google. Any questions you have are at your fingertips. She's already been fixed and given a clean bill of health from the vet."

"When did you set all this up?" I asked, stroking a hand down the kitten's back.

"I went and picked her up yesterday. She spent the night at the vet and is ready for her new home."

"What should I name her?" I asked, holding her up so I could look in her cute squished face.

"Whatever you want. She's all yours."

"What's your cat's name?"

He laughed. "Fred."

"Fred?"

"Yeah, like Fred Flintstone. I'm a huge *Flintstones* fan."

"I've heard of the cartoon, but I've never seen it," I admitted.

"That makes my heart weep," he said, clutching his chest dramatically. "I will have to rectify that."

"Okay, so what's a girl name from the show?"

"Fred's wife's name is Wilma."

"Wilma?" I asked with disbelief. "Are you a Wilma?" I asked the kitten, who gave a plaintive meow.

"Sounds like she likes it to me."

"Wilma it is," I said, setting her back on my lap.

"I'm going to go get the rest of her stuff; that way she can explore the cottage and know where her litter box is," Nathan said, patting Wilma on the head before heading back outside.

We had a little time before we had to leave, so Wilma and I got to know each other. She was a smart kitten and showed off by using her litter box as soon as I placed her in it.

"We better head out," Nathan finally said, glancing at his watch.

"Is it okay to leave her?" I asked worriedly.

"Cats are amazingly self-sufficient. I bet she'll sleep the whole time we're gone and then keep us up half the night trying to play," he said, wrapping his arms around me from behind. "Besides, if we don't head out, I may have to dine on your appetizing neck," he said, placing a kiss there.

"Hmmm, I'm not sure if I should be flattered or not, being compared to food," I said, laughing as I stepped out of his arms. "Besides, you already promised me a movie, so your meal will have to wait. I already perused the showtimes and have the perfect chick flick picked out for us to see," I teased, grabbing my purse and cell phone off the couch. I ran my hand over Wilma's back one last time where she was curled up asleep in a ball on my couch.

"That's fine. I can think of plenty of things I could do to you in a dark theater," he threw my way, making me stumble as pictures of what he could do also filled my head.

He laughed at my expression, linking his fingers through mine. "Kidding. I'm sure the other people watching the movie wouldn't appreciate us putting on our own show, but it is fun to think about what we could do if we did have a theater to ourselves," he added.

"Have you ever?" I asked, morbidly curious about his past experiences.

"Done it in a theater?" he asked, opening the vehicle door.

I nodded, climbing in and buckling my seat belt.

"No, and until you, I never even had the thought," he said, closing the door on my startled expression.

The forty-mile drive to the theater passed quickly as Nathan peppered me with questions about my childhood. He steered clear of anything painful that involved my mom and instead focused on what high school had been like for me. I skirted around my illness and filled him in on what it had been like before I'd gotten sick, back when I thought my toughest problem was trying out for the cheerleading squad. I was still answering his endless questions when he pulled into the parking lot of the theater.

"So, what chick flick did you pick?" he asked.

"The one with the horse," I said innocently, pointing to a poster where a young girl was hugging the neck of a black stallion.

"Really?" he asked.

"Sure. Why, does it not look good to you?" I asked, trying to not snicker and give myself away.

"Almost as good as getting a root canal," he said, studying the poster hard as if he were hoping to find a demon hiding in it or something that would at least redeem it a little.

I doubled over laughing at the expression on his face. "I was kidding," I said between my peals of laughter. "I want to see the spy movie," I said when I was finally able to talk clearly.

"You think you're funny?" he asked, wrapping his arms around me and twirling me around.

"If you could have seen your face," I said, laughing again. "It was classic."

"Funny for you. Meanwhile, I was wondering if I poked my eye out if you would still make me watch it," he said, heading for the ticket booth.

"Lucky for you, I've never been into fluffy movies like that either."

"That's a relief," he said, purchasing two tickets.

Much to my disappointment, the movie I picked was a little more crowded than I would have expected for a Friday afternoon. We found a couple of seats together, sandwiched between two elderly couples. Nathan smiled at me wryly as we took our seats; obviously he was disappointed also.

Nathan held my hand throughout the movie, stroking his fingers across the back of my hand in a seemingly innocent way, except for the fact that I couldn't help thinking about where else his fingers had stroked me. Eventually, though, I lost myself in the twists and turns in the plot of the film.

"What did you think?" he asked once the credits were rolling across the screen and the house lights had been turned on.

"Despite the lack of horses, it was good," I joked, making my way down the steps toward the exit.

He laughed. "Oh yeah, I was quite disappointed no horses needed to be saved."

"Not to mention, there was hardly any bicycle riding," I quipped as he laughed again even harder.

"True, and no trunks with boobies in them," he said loudly, earning him a glare from the older couple that had been sitting beside him. "Too loud?" he asked me as they brushed past us, obviously disgusted with our conversation.

"Maybe a bit," I laughed.

"What time is Tressa expecting us?" he asked, glancing at his watch as we stepped out of the theater.

"Around eight," I said, zipping up my jacket against the wind that had the snow from the ground swirling. "You think Wilma is okay?" I asked, already more attached to the kitten than I probably should be.

"I bet a hundred bucks she's still sleeping where we left her," he reassured me, reaching for my hand to help me step over one of the snowdrifts. "It's a little after six now, so we have time for a bite to eat. Do you have a preference?" he asked, changing the subject.

"Pretty much anything."

"How about steak?" he asked, plugging the information into the GPS on his phone.

"That works," I said, climbing into the vehicle.

"Great. It says there's a steak restaurant right up the road."

The restaurant was busy since it was a Friday night, so we chose to eat at one of the small round tables in the bar area.

"What can I get you to drink?" a short-skirted waitress asked.

"Can I get a rum and Coke?" I asked.

"ID?" she asked, not looking up from her pad.

Ignoring Nathan's grin, I reached into my purse and pulled out my wallet. She glanced at it briefly before handing it back. "You?" she asked, turning to Nathan.

"Vodka on the rocks."

"ID," she said again, making me chuckle.

"Seriously?" Nathan asked.

"Don't take it personally. I card anyone who looks younger than fifty," she said, smiling at us for the first time.

"Don't mind him. He thinks he exudes maturity and wisdom," I said dryly.

"Compared to the immature idiots I've dated, that's not a bad thing. I'd hold on to this one if I were you. He sounds like a keeper to me."

"Why do I suddenly feel like livestock?" Nathan asked as the waitress headed toward the bar to put in our drink order.

"Well . . ." I started to say as my phone chirped, letting me know I had a text. It was from Tressa, checking to see if we were still coming. Her nerves were obviously getting the best of her. *See you soon*, I typed back before stowing my phone in my bag.

"Your friend?"

"Yeah. She was just checking to make sure we were still coming," I said as the waitress returned with our drinks and took our dinner order.

"Whatever happened to your other friend? The one who was at the bar with you the night we met?"

"Brittni? She's at a teaching conference in Seattle until Monday."

"Really? I wouldn't have pegged her for a teacher."

"I said the same thing when I first found out, but supposedly, she's like the kid whisperer or something. Personally, I think she scares them into listening," I joked. "She's definitely different. I think she was burned by some guy a few years back. Ironically, it was when she was in school in Seattle. Tressa did tell me she wound up transferring here at the end of her sophomore year. She's a bit intense, but still awesome," I said, suddenly feeling awkward at the way he was studying me. "Do I have something on my face?"

"No, nothing like that. I just like how your face lights up when you talk about your friends. You obviously like them a lot," he answered as our waitress returned to the table with our dinner.

"I do. They both welcomed me with open arms," I said,

digging into my dinner while he continued to study me. "Aren't you hungry?" I asked.

"I have something I need to tell you first," he said, looking more serious than I had ever seen him.

"Okay. Should I be worried?"

"First, I need to tell you what this week has meant to me," he said just as my phone rang.

Talk about saved by the bell. I wasn't sure if I wanted to hear what he had to say. I answered my phone without taking my eyes from Nathan's. I had to swallow a sudden lump in my throat before I could speak.

"Hello," I finally managed.

"I need you to come now," Tressa whispered into the receiver.

"What?" I asked, not sure I heard her right.

"You have to come now. The date is a complete disaster. I need you to come smooth it over," she pleaded.

"Seriously? What have you done to my confident friend who's not afraid of anything?" I asked her as Nathan's lips quirked at my question.

"She's gone," she hissed into the receiver. "Hurry, please," she demanded before abruptly hanging up on me.

"What was that about?" Nathan asked.

"Tressa. She's totally freaking out. She wants us to come now. Do you mind?" I asked, trying to ignore where our conversation had been going before my phone had interrupted it.

"Nah. I still owe her for the other night," he said, signaling our waitress for the check.

The waitress brought us to-go boxes with the check, not commenting on the sudden departure. Whatever Nathan had been about to say was forgotten as we headed to the small club where we were supposed to meet Tressa and her date. I certainly wasn't going to bring it up. I just wanted to put it out of my mind as we made our way through the smoky room looking for Tressa.

"Ashton, over here," a voice called out to our left as we were halfway to the bar.

"I'm so glad you made it," she said, giving me an exuberant hug that seemed a little too forced.

"You okay?" I whispered in her ear.

"No. I'm a complete wreck. I'm sure he thinks I'm a total assface," she whispered before releasing me. "Ashton, I'd like you to meet Greg. Greg goes to school with me. Greg, this is my friend Ashton and her friend Nathan," Tressa said in a rush, trying to get all the introductions out in one breath.

"Nice to meet you, man," Nathan said, reaching past me to shake Greg's hand.

"Same here," Greg answered, pumping Nathan's hand before releasing it and reaching for mine. "Ashton, I've heard all about you," Greg said, sliding back in the booth next to Tressa after running his eyes down my frame before settling on my breasts. I rolled my eyes.

"Really?" I asked, sliding in across from Tressa.

"Yeah, I was telling him about your bucket list," Tressa said, biting back a yelp when I kicked her under the table. She clammed up immediately. Greg, unfortunately, who was oblivious to my silent insistence, took up where she'd left off.

"It seems pretty fucked up to me," he said, taking a drink. I resisted the urge to kick him also. "I expected you to be all decked out in black, all morbidlike. Don't get me wrong, some Goth chicks are hot," he added.

"Your list is a bucket list?" Nathan asked, looking confused.

"It's for a paper I plan on writing," I lied, wishing the floor would open up and swallow me.

"Yeah, some kind of thesis thing," Tressa interjected, trying to be helpful, knowing she'd put her foot in her mouth. "So, what movie did you guys see?" she asked as Nathan continued to study me.

Keeping my eyes averted from his, I went into a lengthy discussion about the movie, hoping to keep the conversation from returning to my list. I doubted he would figure out the true nature of the significance of the list, but a nagging voice in my head kept taunting me, reminding me he was a reporter. If he tried hard enough, he'd be able to connect all the dots. I would have to tell him the truth before he figured it out.

"Shit, I guess we don't need to go see it," Greg quipped after I finished describing the movie.

"Oops, sorry. I guess I went a little overboard," I apologized, even though I really wasn't sorry. As long as the conversation was far from my list, I was happy.

"It's all good. We probably wouldn't have seen it anyway. It sounds boring. More of an older people flick. No offense," he said, turning toward Nathan.

"None taken," Nathan said dryly, signaling the waitress for a drink as I stifled a laugh.

"So, Greg, what's your major?" I asked, changing the subject.

"I'm a psych major. My dad's been a shrink forever, and that's where the bucks are. The money almost makes up for having to hear people whine all day long," he answered, downing the rest of his beer. "Hey, babe, can I get another brewski?" he interrupted the waitress as she was taking Nathan's drink order.

"No problem," she said, shooting him a you're-a-total-douchebag look. I couldn't have agreed with her more. I couldn't believe that Tressa had somehow managed to find a bigger asshole than Jackson.

As the evening dragged on, it became clear my instincts about Greg were dead-on. He was the typical loudmouth, thinking everything he said was either witty or insightful words of wisdom. He was way off target on both. He was like the thing that wouldn't shut up. By the time we were on our third drink, I had decided that a Brazilian bikini wax while I had electric shock treatments to the eyes would have been less painful.

"I need to go to the bathroom," I told Nathan, shooting Tressa a meaningful look.

"Oh, me too," she said, catching my hint.

Greg said something derogatory under his breath as he slid out of the booth so Tressa could get out.

We weaved our way through the crowd, around a bunch of frat boys who were already past the toasted stage. Several of them called after us, but we ignored them as we made our way to the bathroom.

"What the hell?" I whirled around on Tressa, who looked a faint shade of green. "I thought when you called we were rushing over to make sure your date was running smoothly. What a complete dick."

"I know," she wailed. "Seriously, he's never been an asshole like this in class. I swear, I must have a welcome mat for jerkoffs tattooed on my forehead. I only seem to attract these kinds of guys. Maybe this is the best I'll ever do," she said, sounding close to tears.

"Are you kidding? You can do way better. Okay, I'm not going to lie. You seem to have a way of finding guys who don't match your personality, but we just need to change that. First things first: Your date with Captain Jackass out there is over."

She looked at me incredulously.

"What?" I asked, wondering if I'd stepped over the invisible friendship line and pissed her off.

"Nothing. I've just never seen you like this. Usually you seem so even-tempered. You're almost a badass."

"When it comes to my friends, you should know, I can be a complete bitch. It was all I could do to bite my tongue when you were with Jackson, but I knew there was a history there. You don't owe this monkey-ball-licker out there anything. I—"

My next words were cut off as she threw her arms around my neck. "I seriously love you. I'm so glad you moved here," she said, giving me a smacking kiss on the cheek.

"I love you too, but I don't swing from that tree," I teased, linking my elbow through hers. "Let's go get you out of this date from hell."

Neither of the guys were talking by the time we reached the table. I had the distinct impression that wasn't the case the whole time we were gone. Judging by the scowl on Greg's face and the smirk of satisfaction on Nathan's, something had gone down in our absence.

"We have to go," I said to Nathan, keeping my arm linked through Tressa's. "Tressa's not feeling good," I lied. Nathan jumped up without hesitation, obviously eager to leave.

"What the fuck? Your friends show up and you're suddenly ready to bail," Greg said, reaching out to snag her wrist. "I'm not ready for the night to be over."

"I am. This was a joke," she said with some of the fire I was used to seeing as she jerked her wrist from his hand.

Tressa and I grabbed our purses and turned to leave with Nathan trailing behind us.

"I'm proud of you," I said, giving her a one-armed hug as we headed across the dance floor toward the exit.

"Yeah, but now I have to face him twice a week in class. That ought to be fun," she said sarcastically.

"He'll probably ignore you," I said as someone stepped in front of us, abruptly cutting us off. I was startled to see that it was Greg.

"Babe, don't leave. We were just starting to have fun before your friends showed up," he cajoled, shooting a disdainful look my way. "Stay for a while," he pleaded, grabbing her wrist again.

"Look, Greg, you're a nice enough guy, but I just don't see things working for us," Tressa said, tugging on her hand.

"Why, because your morbid bitch friend shows up and convinces you to leave?" he snarled, tightening his hold on her wrist.

His comment seemed to start a ripple effect. Tressa might allow guys to treat her like a doormat, but she was obviously over it. She thrust her knee up into the poor bastard's groin, just as a fist streaked out from behind us, connecting with his jaw. Greg dropped at our feet in a matter of seconds after the confrontation had started.

The funny thing is no one around us seemed to miss a beat as they continued to dance around Greg lying on the floor. We didn't stick around for questions as Nathan propelled Tressa and me out of the club.

"Dude, your fist came out of nowhere," Tressa crowed as we stepped out into the brisk night.

Nathan merely nodded, not saying anything. It was hard for me to get a read on whether he was mad at Greg for his comment or at himself for hitting him.

"You both were pretty awesome coming to my defense like that," I said, trying to smooth things over.

"As if I'd let some dick talk smack about one of my besties," Tressa said, glancing at Nathan, who was walking several paces ahead of us. She sent me a questioning look, but I shrugged. This brooding side of him was something new to me.

"You just have to remember that attitude if he tries to give you any shit at school," I said, acting like everything was fine.

"I will. Something in there made me snap. I'm not going to

be a doormat anymore. I want a relationship where the guy is willing to punch some dude in the face to defend my honor," she said, making it clear that Nathan could do no wrong in her eyes now.

It was on the tip of my tongue to tell her Nathan and I weren't in a relationship, that what we had was nothing but sexual. I could have set her straight, but even I was unsure what we suddenly were now. We'd been inseparable for the last five days, sharing stories, discovering each other's bodies, and, most of all, forming a bond I don't think either of us was expecting. I wanted him to forget his past history with love, but also, I didn't want to be sick, so we could have a chance at a real relationship.

"I think we should follow you to Woodfalls," Nathan told Tressa, opening her car door for her. "I don't think Greg will be going anywhere soon, but I'd rather you were out of Dodge if he tries to retaliate."

"I don't think he will, but it makes me feel better knowing you guys will be following me," she said as he closed the car door and led me across the lot to where we had parked.

"That was sweet of you," I said, climbing into the vehicle.

"I'm just trying to clear my conscience, since I'm the one who punched him," he said regretfully.

I waited until he started the vehicle and was merging onto the highway before I acknowledged his comment. At first, I debated not bringing it up since he was tightly clutching the steering wheel. "So, I'm glad you were there to help us with that asshole," I finally said. "I'm sure he still doesn't know what hit him," I added, remembering the dazed expression on Greg's face.

"I shouldn't have hit him. He's nothing but a punk-ass kid. I'm past this kind of shit," he muttered more to himself than to me. "And yet, I wish I had hauled his ass outside and kicked it," Nathan answered, closing the gap between Tressa's car and us.

"I'm sure Tressa appreciates your chivalry."

"I didn't punch that sniveling shit for Tressa," he said, finally looking over at me.

"You didn't?" I asked as he reached over and grasped my hand.

"No, sweets. I punched him because of what he said to you. To tell you the truth, I wanted to knock his fucking teeth down his throat. I had to remind myself he's nothing but a stupid kid," he said with the same edge in his voice. It was hard for me to gauge if he was still mad at Greg or if something else was bothering him.

"He's not much younger than me," I reminded him.

"Believe me, I realize that, but the maturity level isn't even close. Sometimes you act like you're older than even Fran, like you've got one foot in the grave. Of course, I think Fran is more honest," he said with bitterness, not looking at me. At that moment, I knew he had figured out my secret.

I turned away from him, glancing out the window, willing myself not to cry. This wasn't a breakup. In order to be a breakup we had to be something that we weren't. This was nothing but a parting of ways.

We drove in silence for several more miles before he asked the question I'd been dreading the most. "Your list is a bucket list?"

"Yeah," I answered, still looking out the window so I wouldn't have to see what he was thinking.

"You're sick?" he asked quietly.

"Yes."

"Cancer? Like your mom?"

"Yes. When I was seventeen I had ovarian cancer. They went in and removed both ovaries in the first surgery. Then, a few months later, they went in and removed my uterus. I was in remission up until four months ago," I answered in a dead voice.

"Are you dying?" he asked, sounding strained.

"Most likely," I said as a hot tear streaked down my face.

"What are your doctors saying?"

"They don't know. I left without telling anyone. Cancer ripped my mom away from my father, and then seven years later it threatened to take me too. We fought it. I lost my hair and nearly my life from the poisonous toxins they were pumping into my body to fight it. It took a toll on my father. I couldn't do it to him again, so I left," I said as he turned the vehicle down the narrow dirt road leading to my house.

I jumped out of the vehicle as soon as he put it in park. I couldn't stand the oppressiveness a second longer. I couldn't and wouldn't have this conversation closed up in a space I couldn't get out of.

I was halfway to my front door when he snagged my hand. "Why didn't you tell me?" he asked, putting his hands on my shoulders to hold me in place.

"I didn't want your pity," I whispered, looking up into his face for the first time.

"Pity? Sweetheart, I don't pity you. I'm too scared to feel anything. You have to go to a doctor. What if you're wrong and it's not back?"

"It's back. I feel it."

"Even more reason for you to go to a doctor," he pleaded. "Why would you run away?"

"Because I knew I couldn't fight it again. It swooped in and snatched my mom right before my eyes and tried to do the same to me. It won't rest until it takes what it wanted all along. Why fight something I was never going to win?"

"You act like it's a living, breathing thing that's out to get you. It's a disease that can be fought," he said, shaking my shoulders slightly for emphasis. "You have to fight it."

"Why?" I asked, waiting for the words that only he could utter that would make me at least try.

"Because I—"

Whatever he had been about to say was cut off as we both took in the black sedan that pulled into my driveway and came to a stop. My heart jumped to my throat as I saw the slightly rumpled, disheveled-looking gentleman step from the vehicle.

Nathan muttered something beside me, but I was focused on the familiar person in front of me.

"Hello, baby," the man greeted me.

"Hi, Daddy," I said as he turned to Nathan.

"Perhaps you'd like to tell me what you're doing seducing the person I hired you to find," he said with contempt in his voice.

24. *The Truth Is Out*

NATHAN

"You were hired to find me?" Ashton asked.

"Yes. I'm a private investigator," I answered, ignoring her father. "I was hired a month ago to locate you and report your whereabouts."

"He took his sweet time to contact me, though, since according to the motel attendant, he's been in town more than a week," her dad blustered.

She held up her hand to silence her father. Her father, the client. That was a fact I hadn't known until tonight. When I took a job, I didn't ask and didn't care who the client was or why he or she wanted someone found. I completed the task because that was all it ever was. The details didn't matter. Everything suddenly made sense. Of course it had to be her father who hired me. It was never a jilted ex-lover like I had assumed.

"You were hired to find me?" she repeated. "And yet you waited to tell my father. Why?"

I knew the moment she figured it out when her eyes clouded over with hurt and her shoulders slumped in defeat.

"You wanted a piece of ass first," she said, cheapening what we had shared. "I'm such an idiot," she continued with disgust.

"No," I said loudly. "You're forgetting who started this affair."

"That's not fair. You're forgetting who stalked who. At the bar. At the bridge. You charmed me into thinking you were actually interested in me!" she shouted, oblivious to the fact that she was airing our dirty laundry in front of her father.

"I was interested in you," I ground out through gritted teeth. "I'm still interested in you," I said, reaching for her.

She looked at my outstretched hand hesitantly before jerking away.

"You lied to me too," I reminded her. "You neglected to tell me you were sick and had run away from home," I goaded her, letting my own frustration get the best of me.

"You're right. I have no right to judge you," she said, brushing a tear away. "No attachments, right? That was the deal," she said, heading for her cottage.

I stood on the porch as her words hit me like a fist to the gut.

"I would trounce you for seducing my daughter if I weren't convinced she just did it for me," her father said, making his way across the porch.

His hand was on the doorknob when my words stopped him. "She's sick," I said as despair crawled its way up my throat.

"I know," he said, his own shoulders drooping. "I knew it the moment she left. She's always been so goddamn worried about what her sickness will do to me. It's partially my fault. I was a mess when we lost her mother. Ashton was left to pick up the pieces and make us a family again even though we were missing such an important piece. We were finally learning to live without her when Ashton got sick," he added, turning to face me.

"She's convinced the cancer won't rest until it takes her," I said, repeating her words from earlier. "She doesn't want to fight it."

"I could see her thinking that. It nearly took her the last time. Sometimes, when I saw the intense pain she was in, I almost wished the cancer would win so she wouldn't feel the pain anymore."

"What are you going to do now?" I asked, frightened by the defeat in his voice. The thought that he was taking her home so she could die scared me beyond belief.

"I'm going to leave the decision to her, but I'm going to stay by her side whatever she decides."

"You have to make her fight," I said with a ragged edge in my voice.

"Why?"

"Because I love her," I admitted, expecting him to tell me I was crazy.

"I suspected as much, which is why I didn't shove your nuts down your throat for touching her," he said, turning away from me. "Despite your delay, I'm thankful you found my daughter," he added, stepping into the cottage and closing the door behind him.

I stood looking at the door for several moments, fighting the urge to storm in and rage at Ashton for giving up. Instead, I forced myself to walk away. I would come back in the morning and tell her our no-attachments deal was void, that I was 100 percent attached. I would make her see reason so she would know I would be at her side, fighting along with her. Tomorrow everything would look better.

I was wrong.

Ashton's car and the sedan from the airport were gone when I arrived at the cottage the next morning after a sleepless night. My fears were confirmed when I peered in the living room window and saw that all of her personal belongings were gone. She'd left without saying anything. Maybe our affair had been nothing to her. Was it possible all my feelings were completely one-sided? She'd warned me not to fall in love with her, claiming one of us would get hurt. Considering it was my chest that felt like a hole had been ripped out of it, I was guessing I was the one in this scenario.

I left her cottage in pain, berating myself for allowing another woman to rip out my heart and stomp on it. This was why I had set my rules. Rules that should never be broken. I returned to the motel and methodically began to pack my personal items. I left the pictures on the wall until the end, intending to tear them up and throw them away since I no longer needed them. I couldn't bring myself to do it. I took each picture down with painstaking care before stowing them carefully in my briefcase. Twenty minutes after entering my room, I was on the road, heading out of town. I looked forward to the long drive home. It would give me time to get my head back on straight.

Passing through town, I saw Fran's store up on the left. I had every intention to continue to drive by. There was no reason to prolong my agony, but my vehicle seemed to have a mind of its own as I turned into the dirt parking lot. It wasn't until I was standing in front of the store that I realized it was closed. I turned back toward my vehicle when a voice called my name. Fran approached me, squinting in the bright sunlight reflecting off the snow-covered ground.

"I was just on my way to come see you," she said, finally reaching my side.

"You would have missed me. I'm headed out."

"Then I'm glad you stopped by before you left. Ashton stopped by this morning on her way out of town. She left something for you," she said, extracting a letter from the pocket of her apron.

"Did you know?" I asked, reaching for the envelope.

"About the cancer?"

I nodded.

"Yes. Ashton confided her secret to me when she applied for the job. I guess working in a general store in some hick town was on that list of hers. She told me I didn't even have to pay her, she'd just be grateful to be able to mark it off her list.

Of course, turns out it was me who was grateful," she said gruffly. "I took to that girl almost immediately. I'll miss her," she added, swallowing hard.

"Me too," I said, shoving the letter in my jacket pocket. "It was a pleasure to meet you, Fran," I added, reaching to shake her hand.

"I don't shake hands with family," she said, pulling me in for a hard hug. "You give my girl time. She'll tell you when she's ready to face her feelings for you."

I nodded, though I was doubtful.

"You come back and see me someday," she said, turning to leave. "And bring that girl's handsome father with you," she added with a smile.

I waited until she was back in her house before I headed back to my vehicle with the letter burning a hole in my pocket. I drove past the Woodfalls welcome sign, unable to believe it had been just over a week ago that I had driven by it the first time. Merging onto the highway, I ignored the letter in my pocket that taunted me every mile I put between Woodfalls and me. Several hours later, I finally pulled off the highway into a rest stop that had been placed in the middle of a wooded area. I reached in my pocket and pulled out the letter, opening it slowly.

Nathan,

How do you write a Dear John letter to someone who changed your life so completely in one short week? I've spent the entire night wondering how I would ever be able to tell you how sorry I am for hiding the truth from you. I thought if I kept things casual neither of us would get hurt. I was wrong. You were right about me. I've been so scared of facing the sickness again. I was scared if I decided to fight, it would win in the end anyway. What I wasn't counting on was meeting someone who would give me a reason to fight it. Someone who would change the way I looked at things, someone who would make me believe in love even when facing mammoth obstacles. So I'm going to fight. All I ask is that if my feelings aren't one-sided that you wait to come to me. Wait for me to fight it. I plan on beating it again but if I don't, I can't stomach having you watch me die. If you feel anything for me, I ask that you respect my wishes.

Love with all my heart today,
tomorrow, for the rest of my life,
Ashton Garrison

25. *Going Home*

ASHTON

The drive back to Florida was bittersweet for me. My dad decided to drive with me, which gave us a chance to catch up. It wasn't until we were able to finally talk that I realized how much I'd missed him. It shocked me to learn he never believed my letter and had known all along I was sick. I knew my absence had hurt him, but he did not try to make me feel bad about it. He expressed that he was glad I was finally able to do something that made me happy. He worked to keep the conversation flowing so that each mile we put between Woodfalls and us wouldn't hurt as much, but no amount of talking could ease that pain. Saying good-bye to Fran and Tressa had been heartbreaking, even with Fran trying to make me laugh through my tears by hitting on my dad.

"Please make sure you call Brittni. She's gonna be crushed knowing she wasn't here when you left," Tressa pleaded.

"I will," I promised. "You stay away from assholes. They don't deserve you," I whispered as she pulled me in for a hug. She tried to wipe the tears from her cheeks to no avail.

I turned to Fran, who held out her arms. "Thank you for everything," I said.

"Honey, I should be thanking you," she replied. "But I want you to do something for me. Fight. Fight hard. If anybody can beat this, I know it's you. I believe it in my heart."

After swearing to them both that I would come back for a visit when I "beat the cancer's ass"—Tressa's words, not mine—we loaded up in my car and drove out of town. The hardest part was leaving without saying good-bye to Nathan. Tears had cascaded down my cheeks as my father steered the vehicle onto the highway, leaving Woodfalls and Nathan behind. Writing the letter had of course been another cowardly act on my part. I had stood at the window the previous evening listening to my father and Nathan's conversation. My heart had stuttered before racing out of control when Nathan professed his love for me. At that moment, I knew I would try to fight the cancer, but I couldn't ask him to stand by me if in the end I lost.

Wilma was actually the thing that wound up distracting me from my grief. She made it known right off the bat that she didn't like the carrier we had picked up for her to ride in. We'd barely been on the highway for ten miles when I eventually caved and let her out. Placing her on my lap, I was relieved when she immediately calmed down and curled up in my lap and promptly fell asleep. She was the comfort I needed as I stroked a hand over her furry back.

The trip home was longer than I remembered. I chalked it up to the frequent kitty bathroom breaks. By the time we'd been on the road for a few days, I was sick of hotels and just ready to be home. I felt completely exhausted. I did none of the driving, but even watching the changing landscapes from state to state had become taxing. My dad insisted on driving the entire time. I tried to argue, but the truth is I was grateful. Wilma continued to sleep on my lap, so I let her stay out of her carrier the entire trip. Each mile that separated Nathan and me weighed heavily on me. It seemed impossible to miss someone as much as I missed him. It went beyond the sexual connection we shared. I missed the conversations we shared and how we seemed completely in sync with each other. Maybe all of that had just been an illusion since he was trying to get close to me, but something inside me told me otherwise. By the time we arrived back home, my brain was a muddled mess and I no longer knew what I should believe.

We arrived back in Florida on a balmy eighty-degree day, and I acutely missed the cooler temperatures in Maine. Wilma and I settled into my father's house since I had given my apartment up when I had left four months ago. I left my boxes in storage, seeing no point in dragging them out until we knew what we were facing.

Two days after arriving home, I was back at the one place I'd wished I would never have to visit again.

"Ashton, I hear we may have a problem?" Dr. Davis said, entering the room where I was perched atop a paper-covered exam table wearing nothing but a smock.

"I think so," I said as he washed his hands in the small sink.

"Symptoms?" he asked with his back to me.

"Fatigue, loss of appetite, aches and pains, and sleepiness," I parroted, fidgeting on the table.

"And you've had these symptoms how long?" he asked, putting his stethoscope to my chest.

"Four and half months," I admitted, waiting for his ridicule.

"I see," he clucked. "Are they the same now or worse?"

"Worse," I answered as he checked my lymph nodes with his fingers.

"Fever?"

"Once, but I think it was just a cold," I answered, fighting to keep my thoughts away from thinking about how Nathan had taken care of me during the fever.

"Possibly, but it could be a sign of something more serious, as I'm sure you're aware of," he said, finishing his exam.

"It's back," I stated.

"I don't like to fry the egg before it's hatched, but your symptoms are troublesome. I also don't like the lump I felt under your right arm. The first step is to do some blood work and biopsy the lump," he said, patting my leg. "You get dressed while I fill out the paperwork. We've fought it before, we'll fight it again."

I nodded, accepting his words. In one swoop, he'd crushed

the little bit of hope I had been harboring that I was wrong. I knew the blood work and biopsy were just a formality.

"Are you going to call Nathan?" my father asked when I told him.

I shook my head no before heading to my room before my tears could fall. I found it ironic that for years I had no problem keeping the tears at bay, and now with the mention of one name, I was a mess.

My predictions proved to be true as the results from the blood work and biopsy came in. The lump under my arm was taken out, and I was scheduled to start chemotherapy immediately. Dr. Davis was confident that even though the lump was large, they were able to remove all the cancer cells, but he wanted to treat it with an aggressive round of chemotherapy. Again, my father asked if I was going to call Nathan, but again, I resisted. A week after returning home, I was at the chemo clinic getting my first regimen of chemotherapy. The bitterness I expected to feel when they injected the needle in me was missing. My desire to fight for Nathan made each step that much more important. Instead of viewing the chemo as poison, I looked at it as a lifeline that would help me reach my goal. My optimism didn't change as I kneeled before the toilet puking up everything I ate. I pretended it didn't hurt when the first large chunk of hair fell out while I was brushing my hair. I didn't allow myself to dwell on how I'd been growing my hair out for the last four years, or how Nathan's hands had felt tangled in the strands. Wilma became a source of comfort

I would have never thought possible. By October, all my hair was gone and I had lost ten pounds, which made my cheekbones stand out in an alarming way. Thanksgiving was spent in the hospital when my immune system decided to stop working. My time in the hospital floated by in a pain-filled haze as I fought to stay alive. Throughout it all, my father never left my side. He didn't mention calling Nathan this time, knowing this was what I had been trying to spare both of them from witnessing. At one point, in my painkiller-hazed state, I dreamt that Nathan was with me. Even at death's door, I was bitterly disappointed that the dream had to end. I was conscious enough when Dr. Davis told my father to prepare himself for the worst, and still, I fought, willing my body not to give up. Perhaps it was the dream that gave me the will to fight harder. Three days after Thanksgiving, I was well enough to be wheeled out of ICU and taken to a regular room.

"How's my favorite patient?" Dr. Davis said, entering my room the day after I'd been moved from the ICU.

"You only say that because I'm the most stubborn," I joked weakly.

"You are one tough nut," he said, sitting in the chair next to my bed. "So, how are you feeling?"

"Fair," I lied, smiling slightly.

He chuckled. "Does 'fair' now stand for being hit by a cement truck?"

I tried to shrug, but even that was too painful.

"I'll have them increase your pain meds. There's no reason you need to suffer unnecessarily," he said, patting my shoulder before standing up. "You have Nurse Ratched call me if you need anything," he added, referring to the head nurse no one liked much.

"That would require me actually talking to her," I quipped, making him laugh as he left my room.

"How you doing, pumpkin?" my dad asked, entering my room with his hands full a few minutes after Dr. Davis had left.

"Fair," I said, giving him my standard answer. "What's all that?"

"I figured a few creature comforts from home would make your stay here easier," he said, setting my iPad on the rolling bed tray. "I brought some of those pajama pants you like to sleep in and a few T-shirts I found in your dresser," he added, placing the stack of clothes on the nightstand.

My eyes zeroed in on the stack of clothes as I spotted a familiar navy blue T-shirt that had been buried at the bottom of my dresser. The fact that he had to dig for it wasn't lost on me, although if he knew the significance of the shirt, he didn't show it. It didn't belong to me, but that didn't stop me from taking it when I had found it in my laundry basket when I packed up my stuff at the cabin. At the time, I had pressed it to my face, smelling the cologne Nathan wore with a touch of his masculinity. When we had arrived home, I had stowed it away and only allowed myself to remove it when the pain of missing him began to engulf me. Everything in me yearned to press it to my face now, but I knew it would raise questions if I asked my father to hand it to me. Not to mention, he would probably think I was a freak if I sniffed my shirt.

"How's Wilma?" I asked.

"She misses you. I debated sneaking her in, but figured Nurse Dictator would have my head if I tried."

"Are you feeding her twice a day?"

"Yes, and giving her those treats you buy that she likes so much. She's been sleeping with me while you've been away," he said sheepishly.

"I'm glad. She likes to snuggle," I said. "Shouldn't you be at work?" I asked as it dawned on me that he was in my room during the middle of the day. "Dad?" I said as he ignored my question.

"I took a leave of absence," he finally admitted.

"Dad, you didn't have to do that," I protested.

"Ashton, we almost lost you this week. How do you think I would have felt if I were at work and something happened to you? Truthfully, I'm debating early retirement. That way I can help take care of you."

"And what will you do when I no longer need to be taken care of?" I asked as some of my optimism returned.

"I'll fish."

"Fish?" I quizzed. "When have you ever wanted to fish?"

"I've recently discovered deep-sea fishing is quite the pastime."

"When have you ever gone deep-sea fishing?" I asked, skeptically.

"I've gone out a couple times with a buddy of mine."

"I didn't know you even liked to fish," I said.

"That's because I really never gave it a chance. I've discovered it can be very relaxing, almost like meditation without all the mumbo jumbo."

"Retirement, though? Won't you get bored? You've always been such a computer nerd."

"I'm ready for a change, and the upside is I'll be there for you," he said.

"Dad, I don't want you to shackle yourself to me," I mumbled.

"Honey, when you were sick before, it somehow became all about me. I allowed my grief and fear of losing your mom to cloud my senses. I burdened you by wearing my grief on my sleeve. Even though you were sick as a dog, you continued to console me. This time it's my turn. I'm going to be the strong one," he said, unfolding my favorite blanket from home and spreading it out over me.

I was touched at his thoughtfulness. He'd always been a good father, making sure all my basic needs were taken care of, but after my mom died, he'd closed himself off emotionally, always keeping me at arm's length. It was a nice feeling for him to be so attentive.

"Thanks, Dad," I said as he tucked the blanket around me. My limited energy melted away and I fell asleep to him smoothing a hand across my hairless head.

26. *Waiting*

NATHAN

I impatiently tapped my fingers against the tabletop, waiting for my lunch date to show up. Waiting had made me short-tempered and I had already alienated the waitress, who was probably spitting in my drink. She should have been used to my mood swings since the restaurant had practically become my home away from home over the last few days. It was far enough away that I wasn't technically breaking the rules, but close enough that I could act at a moment's notice. The harried waitress started to approach my table again, but I waved her off like she was an annoying gnat. I could hear her openly bitching to her fellow waitresses, who all clucked their tongues sympathetically. They'd been on the receiving end of my temper at one time or another during my stakeout. I would have apologized, but at the moment, I cared about only one thing, and if my lunch appointment didn't show up in the next few minutes, I would be taking matters into my own hands.

Two minutes later, I was rising from the table with the intention of leaving when the person I had been waiting for hurried through the restaurant's door.

"You're late," I snapped, sinking back into my seat.

"Sorry, I wanted to wait until she fell asleep," Charles, Ashton's father, apologized, sliding into the seat across from me.

My expression immediately softened. "How is she?" I asked earnestly, waving the waitress away as she approached our table. I took no notice of her glares and grumbling as I focused on the man in front of me.

"She's better," he said in a voice thick with relief.

"Really?" I asked, releasing a pent-up breath I wasn't even aware I was holding.

"Yes. Her doctor said she's on the road to recovery. She has one more round of chemo and then we will see."

"She's really okay?" I asked again, swallowing the sudden lump in my throat. The last few days had been absolute hell. Unbeknownst to Ashton, I had been at the hospital waiting for updates from her father. At one point, when they thought she might not make it, I had stood over her bed, clutching her unconscious hand in my own. I had silently willed her not to give up.

"She really is. Some of her spunk is already returning," he said, chuckling softly.

"What does that mean?" I asked.

"I stuck that shirt of yours in the middle of a stack of clothes I brought to her room. She couldn't take her eyes from it."

"You're a meddling old fool, but I love you for it," I said, grinning at him. I was grateful to Charles for trusting me, for believing that my feelings and intentions for Ashton were real. I had suggested fishing together as a way for us to get to know each other and maybe relieve some of the stress. On one of our fishing trips, he had mentioned the shirt of mine that Ashton had kept. At the time, I'd been struggling with doubts that Ashton still had feelings for me and was beginning to feel like a fool for selling my condo and moving across the state so I could be closer to her. As October melted into November, her silence had begun to wear on me.

"So she stared at the shirt. That may not mean anything," I said.

"You telling me I don't know my own daughter? Don't be an idiot, boy. She's head over heels in love with you."

"Did you bring her the flowers I bought?" I asked, sitting back in my seat.

"Yes, though she thinks they're from me," he grumbled.

"That doesn't matter as long as she got them," I said as our waitress approached our table cautiously.

"I'll have the club sandwich with the fries," I said, placing my order before she could ask. I smiled broadly at her as I handed over my menu.

"And you?" she asked Charles after shooting me a look that pretty much indicated she thought I was crazy.

"When do they think she'll be released?" I asked, pumping him for information once he'd ordered and the waitress had left.

"Her doctor is going to wait until after her last chemo treatment. He wants to make sure her immune system doesn't decide to act up again. Once she's out of the woods, she'll start recovery."

"How does she look?" I asked, unable to shake the image of how she had looked hooked up to all the machines when I had last seen her.

"Rough. It's obvious she's in pain," he said, holding up his palm when I went to interrupt. "I talked to Dr. Davis before I left, and he said he had already put in the order to up her pain medicine," he finished before I could say anything.

"She shouldn't have to be in that much pain," I said through gritted teeth.

He sighed, used to my outbursts by now. "Agreed, and we're taking care of it. We care about her well-being too," he reminded me. "You have to remember, Ashton is very stubborn, and we're trying our best to read between the lines."

I slumped down in my seat as my sudden burst of anger dissipated. I knew he was right. I had seen firsthand just how stubborn Ashton could be. It just frustrated me beyond words that I couldn't be by her side when she needed me the most.

"How's the writing going?" he asked, changing the subject.

"Not bad. Turns out I kind of have a knack for writing stories. The *News Journal* just bought another one of my stories and optioned for the one I'm currently working on. I've also landed a couple online writing jobs. Who knew a lie about a fictional job would turn into something? Of course, I know you had a part in it. Thanks again, Charles."

"All I did was place a call to a friend of mine. The rest was all you."

"We sure have come a long way from you wanting to shove my nuts down my throat," I joked.

"You hurt my girl and you just better hope you can choke them down," he threatened.

I nodded, falling back on the crux of the whole thing. She had asked me to wait and I was trying my damnedest to be patient, but having her so close and not being able to be with her was killing me.

Charles and I finished our lunch in silence. "You'll call me if anything happens," I stated, dropping money on the table to cover the check.

"You know I will. Are we fishing Sunday?" he asked, pulling on his light jacket.

"Do you think it's wise to leave her for a day so you can go off fishing?"

"Boy, this fishing trip isn't for me. I guess you haven't looked in a mirror lately, but trust me when I say you look like hell."

"How's Wilma?" I asked, ignoring his observation as we exited the restaurant together.

"She misses Ashton, but otherwise she still acts like she owns the place."

"Sounds like a typical cat," I said. "I'll see you Sunday as long as you think it's okay to leave her for a day."

"By Sunday she'll be ready to cut off my head if I don't give her a break," he said before crossing the street.

I watched his retreating back for a few seconds as he disappeared through the hospital doors. My steps were noticeably lighter as I rounded the corner to the hospital's parking garage. The last few days had been the worst of my life and had given me a better insight to why Ashton had tried to keep me away. I now knew she was trying to spare me the heartache, but she underestimated my feelings for her. Even after a two-month absence, she still dominated my thoughts. She was my first thought in the morning and the last at night. The note she had left me was nothing but a tattered mess from the countless times I had read it and still, I waited.

I fed Fred when I arrived home before stumbling to my bed and crashing. Four days of sleepless nights had finally caught up to me. I slept through the rest of the day and all that night.

Waking up refreshed the next morning, I placed a call to the hospital and cajoled the nurse into giving me an update on Ashton's status. Pleased to hear that she was on the road to recovery, I got back to my everyday responsibilities, even though the task of trying to take my mind off her was impossible. The rest of the week followed the same routine: wake up, call the hospital, pretend I was a normal human. The only deviations from my schedule were the days I allowed myself to camp out at the diner to work. I was happier on those days. Being close at hand, though, I was beginning to feel like a crazy stalker.

I was working at the diner the following week, sucking down coffee that the waitresses kept filled to the brim, when in a moment of weakness, I had confessed my real reason for constantly being there. The response was immediate. I was no longer the customer they tried to pawn off on one another. Instead, every waitress fought over who would serve me after that.

"Today's when she's being released, right?" Cathy, one of the older waitresses, asked, joining me at the booth they designated as mine. It was a prime location due to the fact that it butted up to the big plate glass window that faced the hospital.

"Yeah," I said, taking a sip of the coffee she'd just topped off. "Charles doesn't know when, though."

"Are you going to talk to her?" she asked, resting the coffeepot on the table.

"No, I'm going to respect her wishes."

"That girl doesn't realize how good she has it. I wish I had a man pining after me. You come look me up if you ever get tired of waiting for her," she joked. I knew she wasn't serious. Our story was common knowledge now and all of them were rooting for us.

The day seemed to pass in slow motion as I waited to catch a glimpse of Ashton as she left the hospital. I kept my phone on the table so Charles could reach me if something had changed. By the time the sun started to set, it became obvious that they had decided not to release her today. Dropping a couple of bills on the table, I headed out of the restaurant decisively. I was sick of waiting for Charles to contact me. I would find out for myself what was going on. Fear was of course clouding my head. What if she'd had a relapse and that was the reason for the silence?

I was halfway across the street, standing on the median, waiting for traffic to let up, when the hospital doors slid open just as the complimentary valet service pulled an ivory-colored Town Car up to the curb. My eyes found those of the frail woman who held my heart in her hands. I saw her eyes widen with surprise and throw a question to her father, who was pushing her wheelchair. I saw him shake his head in denial. Her eyes found mine again, no longer filled with surprise but with horror before they quickly darted away. My heart dropped to my knees as I watched her instruct her father to help her into the car. Within seconds, their car smoothly merged into the oncoming traffic. I stood on the median in disbelief as cars whizzed by me on both sides, but still I remained. In all the times I had fantasized about what our meeting would be like, none of my scenarios had gone like this.

I made my way to my vehicle, paying no attention to the traffic around me or the honked horns or obscene gestures. I was too busy trying to sift through the facts in my head, the most glaring being that I was a fool. I romanticized about a relationship because of some letter, which in hindsight could have been her way of gently letting me go. She obviously never expected me to change my life around for her. I couldn't even blame her for my stupidity. She hadn't asked me to sell my condo and move across the state. All she'd asked was to give her time. It was obvious by the look she'd given me that she'd never expected to see me again. Our time in Woodfalls was exactly what she always said it was. We'd come together with no attachments. It was time for me to accept that it would never be anything more. It was time to move on.

27. Trying to Heal

ASHTON

My emotions were a mess by the time my father pulled into our circular driveway. The ride home had passed in tense silence. I ignored the furtive glances he sent my way throughout the drive. I was too angry to acknowledge them.

It annoyed me that I required his help to get to my room, but my hospital stay had depleted my limited energy supply to a nonexistent level.

"Can I get you anything?" he asked once I was settled on my bed with Wilma.

I shook my head, anxious for him to leave. He started to say something, but thought better of it and walked out of my room. The sob I had been holding back since I saw Nathan bubbled up through me the moment the door closed. I wanted to curse fate that he had seen me at that moment. I cringed at what he must have seen. I was a weak shell of the woman I had been in Woodfalls. My body was frail and ravaged from the sickness that had ripped its way through me, but vainly, it was my head that I was the most ashamed of. Upon my release from the hospital, I'd been expecting to go straight home, so I didn't see any reason to wear a hat or one of the silk scarves that my father had bought me. Without looking in the mirror I knew what my head looked like; all I had to do was smooth a hand over its surface to know. All the auburn hair Nathan had loved was gone. There was nothing left for him to run his fingers through. I could not stand to see the pity in his eyes, so I'd instructed my father to bring me home.

Wilma crawled up onto my chest, rubbing her fur against my tear-stained cheeks, trying to comfort me. I smoothed my hand down her back as she purred her pleasure. "You don't care that I'm a bald skeleton, do you?" I murmured as she continued to purr loudly. "I saw our friend today. He looked amazing," I told her as she continued to rub against me like she totally understood what I was saying. "He's even more handsome than I remembered," I told her softly, knowing she was the only one I could confide in. She was still lying on top of me when I eventually fell asleep with thoughts of Nathan still running through my head on an endless loop.

I felt fractionally more human the next morning when I woke. I made a silent vow not to cry again. It was no use crying over spilled milk. So he'd seen me at my worst. I would make damn sure the next time he saw me I would resemble the woman he remembered rather than the glimpse of the one he'd gotten at the hospital. I would be stronger and no longer sick the next time he saw me.

My father was fixing my breakfast when I joined him. He looked at me warily, obviously trying gauge whether I was holding a grudge. "So, you told Nathan I was in the hospital," I stated.

"Yes," he answered, setting a plate with pancakes in front of me.

"Is he this fishing buddy of yours?" I asked as pieces of the puzzle came together. I remembered a conversation with Nathan where he told me his favorite pastimes were scuba diving and deep-sea fishing.

"Yes," he answered, sitting across from me with his own plate.

"Why didn't you tell me you were friends?" I asked, nibbling at my pancakes. I really wasn't hungry, but eating was the only thing that would help restore my body.

He sighed before answering. "I wanted to, but you seemed so closed off to the subject."

"How long has he been here?" I asked, acknowledging his comment with a small nod of my head.

"Since October."

"So he lives here now?" I asked, ignoring the fluttering in my heart.

"Yes. Are you going to see him?" he asked nonchalantly.

"No," I answered, leaving no room for argument as I forced myself to finish my breakfast.

We didn't speak about Nathan for a long time after that.

Christmas came and went and January bled into February. My body went into semi-remission and the doctors put me on a regimen of medication. They were once again optimistic. I decided against counting the days down to the five-year mark this time. Instead, I measured the days in increments as my body began to recover and my hair began to grow now that I was no longer having chemo treatments. I also joined a gym and slowly began to build my body back up. Ironically, my exercise of choice turned out to be running, which of course reminded me of Nathan every time I stepped on the treadmill. When I wasn't working out, I was interning at the local hospital in the psychiatric department while I waited to get into the master's program I had applied to. My days were full as I worked to keep busy, but no matter how busy I kept myself, thoughts of Nathan were always lurking just below the surface. As my body became stronger, I didn't shove them away, knowing that soon I would see him again. I knew that he doubted my feelings for him by things my father had let slip, but in the end, I would show him just what he meant to me. I would tell him I fought the battle for him.

I should have expected fate to jerk the carpet out from under me since I seemed to be some kind of cosmic joke to it, but when it struck, I was completely unprepared. Ironically, it was me who opened the floodgates.

"How's the fishing been going?" I asked my father casually over breakfast one morning at the end of February.

"Good. Nathan can't go out as much as we'd like now that he's so busy," he said, not looking at me.

"Busy?" I asked, parched for any information about him.

"Yeah, he's been dating this girl he met over at the *News Journal*," he answered, looking unconcerned as he added eggs to my plate.

"Dating?" I asked, not sure I had heard him right.

"Yeah, I guess he finally got the hint that you had moved on."

"Right," I said weakly, not looking up from my plate. I should have known if I continued to push him away he would eventually get sick of waiting. I wasn't even sure I could blame him. Our whole relationship was based on the one week we had shared. It suddenly seemed completely ridiculous that anyone would wait almost six months for someone they really didn't know that well. Chances were he'd discovered what he thought was love was really nothing more than lust during a stressful time. I finished my breakfast in an agony-filled haze before excusing myself from the table.

I didn't cry as I slowly walked to my room, or when I began to get dressed or even when I pulled out his old navy blue T-shirt that I preferred to work out in.

"You okay?" my dad asked as I headed for the front door a few minutes later in my running gear.

"I'm fine," I lied. "I'm going to work out."

"Gym or the beach?" he asked.

"The beach. Why?" I asked, finally focusing on him.

"I just worry when you're running on the beach. Do you have the Mace I bought you?"

I held up my keys so he could see the travel-size Mace that was hooked to them, not mentioning the fact that I always left my keys in the car.

"Be careful," he said, giving me a quick kiss on the cheek.

"I will."

My dad had suggested a different beach that he said was less crowded. I was relieved to find the parking lot relatively empty and silently thanked my father for showing me this particular spot a few weeks back. It was ideal for running since you didn't have to worry about maneuvering around sunbathers or watching out for small children who were prone to dart in front of you. The majority of the properties that lined this beach were privately owned, which kept the beach population at an all-time low. Stowing my keys beneath the driver's seat, I used the keypad on the door to lock the car behind me.

I replayed my father's words as I made my way down the steep staircase leading to the beach below. Away from prying eyes, I stood at the shore for a moment, watching the waves crashing against the shore. The knowledge that Nathan had moved on was crippling, and I fought against the urge to sink down on the sand and weep. Instead, I did the next best thing as far as I was concerned: I took off running down the beach. I pushed myself harder than I had ever before, sprinting along, trying to escape the haunting memories. Only when my vision was threatened by black spots did I finally allow myself to slow. Placing my hands on my knees, I gasped for air, fighting to keep down my breakfast. Once I was sure I wasn't going to die due to lack of air in my lungs, I stood up straight. I was astonished at the distance I had covered after glancing back the way I had just come. Impressive or not, it didn't stop the stitch that had developed in my side. I walked slowly back toward where I had started, watching the incoming waves on the sand. It was nice to have the beach completely to myself, especially since I was a sweaty mess. My short hair was plastered to my head and my clothes were drenched in sweat.

No sooner had that thought entered my head than a lone runner appeared in the horizon. At least it was a fellow runner, who would most likely be so intent on finishing his or her own workout that the person wouldn't notice what I looked like. The gap between us narrowed and after a few minutes, I was able to make out his features. Stopping in the sand, I watched as his eyes widened with surprise when he recognized me and came to a halt.

"Hello, Nathan," I said, pleased that my voice didn't betray me by trembling.

"Ashton," he said, looking like he'd been hit by a brick. "What are you doing here?" he asked, like he owned the beach beneath my feet.

"Getting my nails done," I said sarcastically, suddenly pissed that he was allowed to move on, while I was stuck in limbo. "What does it look like?" I added, indicating the sweat dripping off my body.

He looked taken aback at my sarcasm before his own face hardened. "I see. Well, I'm sorry you were forced to lay eyes on me," he said in the same voice I'd heard him use on Greg months ago. "I know you like to pretend there was never anything between us," he added, turning away.

I watched as he started to jog away as anger swirled up

through me at his gall. He was the one who acted like what we had was nothing. "I think it's awfully rich for you to throw that line at me when you're the one who's moved on," I shouted at his back. His steps faltered and then stopped, but he kept his back to me. "I know asking you to wait was a ridiculous request considering we barely knew each other, but I'd hoped your feelings were the same as mine," I continued to yell as he slowly turned to me.

"What the fuck are you talking about?" he yelled. "I've done nothing but wait for you. I switched jobs, sold my condo, moved across the state, all so I could be closer to you; all on the off chance that you would finally tell me the wait was over. I had to beg like some dog for scraps to get information off your father. I was forced to sit idly by in some diner instead of being by your side while you almost died. I did nothing but wait for you, and then, the one time I actually get to see you, you act like I'm not even there. You treated me like some chump you had a one-night stand with who you would rather never lay eyes on again. You stomped on my heart like a heartless bitch and drove away," he yelled, closing the distance between us in angry strides before stopping right at my face. "How could you act like what we shared was nothing?" he asked before pulling me in for a rough kiss. Time stopped moving as the familiarity of his lips settled against mine. The kiss was filled with anger and hurt, but it did not stop my heart from racing with excitement. "Why?" he whispered, finally pulling back, but not loosening his grip on my shoulders.

"Because I couldn't bear for you to see me like that. I was ashamed. My hair was gone, and I was weaker than an eighty-year-old woman. I wanted to spare you the horror of what I looked like. I was scared that the passion you once felt for me would be replaced with pity. I couldn't face that. I wanted you to remember me the way I was in Woodfalls," I said as a tear escaped my overflowing eyes.

"Pity you? That was your fear, not mine. You were assuming I would feel a certain way without giving me the chance to show you I could have been there for you."

"I just didn't want you to see me die if the cancer beat me."

"So, my last memory would have been of you wanting nothing to do with me?" he returned, sounding frustrated.

"I'm sorry. I thought I was doing what was best for both of us."

"Why didn't you call me when you started to get better?" he asked quietly. It appeared my admission had taken some of the wind from his sails as his anger melted away.

"Vanity. I wanted to have something besides a scarf covering my head," I said, self-consciously rubbing a hand over my short hair, which had grown in darker than its previous shade. "I needed to feel normal," I admitted. "It doesn't matter anymore anyway. It's too late."

"Because you don't love me anymore?" he asked in a resigned voice.

"Of course I do, idiot," I said as a fresh wave of anger flared up inside me. "But my father told me you met someone else," I said, jerking my shoulders from his grasp.

"Charles told you . . ." he asked incredulously before throwing back his head with laughter.

"What the hell is so funny about my father telling me?" I snapped, fighting the urge to slap the grin off his face.

"Your father is a born matchmaker."

"Are you trying to tell me he's the one who set you up?" I asked, feeling the sting of betrayal. "He told me you met her at work."

"Your father didn't set just me up, he set you up too," he said softly, taking my hand in his.

"You're not seeing someone?" I asked as understanding dawned on me.

He shook his head. "Sweets, the only one I want to see is standing in front of me."

"My father set us up. Is that how you knew I'd be here today?" I asked, trying to put all the puzzle pieces together.

"No, but he knows I run here every day."

"That's why he pushed me to come here. No wonder he was so nosy this morning," I mused. "You're not bike riding with some chick from work?" I repeated, sagging in relief. My emotions felt bittersweet as I fully digested everything Nathan had said. I had done us both a disservice by pushing him away and turning my back when I needed him the most. I was acutely disappointed for all the time we'd missed together because of my selfishness. The fact that he hadn't given up on me not only was soothing but filled me with a newfound hope for the future.

He laughed again. "You're the only one I want to bike

with, sweetheart," he said, pulling me to him and resting his lips against mine.

Our lips melded together, filled with tenderness and promises of no anger or hurt. The past was forgotten as we lost ourselves in each other's arms, rediscovering what had brought us together in the first place.

"By the way, your hair is sexy as hell," he whispered in my ear. "Should we let Charles know we found each other, or should we make him squirm?"

"Well, I am still pissed that he lied to me this morning, but on the other hand, it made me face the music. I kept pushing back when I was going to contact you. First, it was after the chemo. Then it was once I went into remission, and then I changed it to when I no longer resembled a bald baby. Truthfully, I think I was just afraid to face you. I was scared that it wouldn't be like it was. Everything happened so quickly before. All the decisions we made were dictated by lust. I was afraid that once we faced reality, that same passion would no longer be there in light of real-life problems."

"That's love, sweetheart. We take the good and the bad."

"This time I want us to take it slow. Really get to know each other and make sure what we share is real. This time, I want to be nothing but attached," I whispered as our lips sealed together.

Epilogue

"I can't believe you're leaving me."

"Dad, you've known for the last two months that I'd be moving out today," I said, hauling a heavy box down the hall, which was proving difficult since Wilma was rubbing against my ankles. "Besides, this isn't the first time I've left home," I said, swiping a bead of sweat off my forehead.

"Yeah, but not hundreds of miles away," he griped, watching me place the box near my suitcase.

"Dad, you know it's not permanent. We'll only be in Woodfalls for the summer," I said for what felt like the hundredth time.

"If I knew he would repay me for playing matchmaker by taking my baby away, I would have rethought my plans," he mumbled as the doorbell rang. "There's the traitor now," he complained as I hurried to the front door.

"Hi," I said, throwing open the front door.

"Hi yourself, beautiful," Nathan said, pulling me into his arms for a quick kiss.

"How's the old man?" he asked, pulling back.

"Grumpy as hell. Do you have his ticket?" I asked.

"Right here," he said, holding up the plane ticket we'd decided to purchase for my father so he could fly to Woodfalls to come see us in July.

"Dad, we have a surprise for you," I said, coming back into the formal living room with the plane ticket in hand.

"Let me guess: You've decided to make the move permanent," he said sarcastically, glaring at Nathan.

"Daddy," I sighed. "Don't be a grouch. We bought you a ticket to come see us in Woodfalls in July. So now you can wipe the scowl from your face."

"You did?" he asked, breaking into a wide grin. "I thought maybe you two wanted to get away from me."

"Oh, Dad," I said, throwing my arms around him. "That's not why we're going to Woodfalls," I said as Nathan chuckled lightly behind me. I pulled away from my dad so I could glare at Nathan, but failed miserably when he winked at me. My insides still liquefied from his wink. Judging by the wicked grin on his face, he was well aware of that fact.

"Let's go," he said abruptly, grabbing my box off the floor and heading out to his Range Rover. I followed behind with Wilma in my arms while my dad dragged along my two suitcases. I placed Wilma next to her new best friend, Fred, on the blanket Nathan had spread across the backseat. "You two be good," I said, petting each of them.

Nathan had already stowed my luggage in the back of the vehicle by the time I closed the car door.

"Sir, I look forward to fishing with you next month," Nathan said, shaking my father's hand.

"Take care of my baby," my father replied, pulling Nathan in for a rough man-hug.

"You can count on it," Nathan said, rounding the vehicle so I could say good-bye in private.

"I love you, Dad," I said, throwing myself into his arms. "Thank you for helping me with everything this year," I added earnestly.

"I'm always here for you. If all goes as planned, for the rest of my life, not yours," he said, squeezing tightly before releasing me.

"I know," I said, smiling at him through my sudden tears. "I'll see you next month," I added, opening my door.

"You two drive safely and call when you get to that hick town," he demanded before closing my door for me.

"We will," Nathan and I answered as the door clicked shut.

"You ready?" Nathan asked, pulling out of my driveway.

"I've been ready for two months," I answered.

"So have I, sweets," he said, not missing my innuendo. "This has been the longest three months of my life," he added, shooting me a wry look.

"Hey, it's been tough for me too," I pointed out. "But we did it," I said, referring to my plan for us to take it slow. We had collectively decided that we would date first. It was important to me that we got to know each other for real this time since our previous relationship had been built on secrets. I had announced that I didn't think we should sleep together again until we had been together for three months. Nathan acted like a sport about it the entire time. Hell, by the end of March, I wished I could have eaten my words.

"A lot of cold showers, that's what's gotten me through it," Nathan suggested.

I was ready to cave a couple times, convinced we had proven my point, but surprisingly, he would remind me of our deal. At first, I began to worry that maybe he didn't want me as much as he used to, but then he sprang his idea of us going back to Woodfalls to celebrate the three-month mark. The idea took hold of me, and the idea of waiting until then almost seemed worth it. We would finally make love where it had all began.

"Do you have your medicine?" he asked.

"Yep," I answered, patting my purse. My sickness was no longer a taboo subject and though I was in semi-remission, we had openly talked about the possibility of a relapse. From the very beginning of getting back together, Nathan had informed me in no uncertain terms that if I did relapse, he wasn't going anywhere. He proved his point by joining me at each of my doctor's appointments and often asking more questions than me. Every so often, I would panic slightly that we were jinxing it by talking about it so much. He had gently reminded me that even before, when I'd bottled it up, it had still returned. "It's better to know what we're facing than to be surprised," he had reasoned.

"How long does it take to get there again?" I asked, checking the GPS map as he merged onto the highway heading north.

"Couple of days, less if I don't stop for food or gas," he joked, reading my thoughts.

"Anxious, are we?"

"Honey, I won't be happy until your legs are wrapped around my waist," he said, placing his hand on my knee. Slowly tormenting each other turned out to be the theme of our trip. All the desire we'd been keeping at bay seemed to pulsate between us with each mile that brought us closer to Woodfalls. Stopping at night was the worst. It's just like running when you can see the finish line, but you're not sure you can make it. We agreed to get adjoining rooms, and it took all my willpower not to sneak over to his room. Only the thought of saving it for the cottage gave me the strength I needed. The days were at least easier since we would distract ourselves by playing silly car games. Other times I would read to him to help whittle the hours away. It was dusk on the third day when we finally drove past the Woodfalls welcome sign. I grinned with pleasure as we drove by Fran's store and Joe's bar, where we had met. Fran and I had kept up a correspondence through email during the past year, and she was excited to see me again. I preferred to chat with Tressa and Brittni on the phone, but I had yet to tell them I was coming and had sworn Fran to secrecy. I wanted to surprise them.

Nathan pulled into the familiar driveway and my heart pinched with happiness at the sight of the cottage. At the moment, I was so happy we had decided to wait. It only seemed right that we would rediscover each other here.

Nathan made quick work of unpacking the Range Rover while I got the cats settled inside.

I stepped out to the porch to see if Nathan needed any help. My heart began to race as he slowly approached with the smile that still melted everything inside me. It felt like forever since we'd last stood on this very same spot together. The last time we were here betrayal and lies had threatened the shaky relationship we had. Now, honesty and love bound us together. What started out as a no-attachments bargain had turned into the love story I thought would never be mine. We had no idea what our future held, but we were certain that as long as we had each other, we could face anything.

"Are you ready?" Nathan asked, reaching for my hand and leading us toward our future—together.

READ ON FOR A SPECIAL PREVIEW OF

Contradictions

A Woodfalls Girls Novel

AVAILABLE DECEMBER 2014 FROM BERKLEY

"Where's Chuck?" Cameo asked, handing me a beer she had snagged from the coolers that lined the floors in the kitchen of the frat house we were hanging out in. The house was Gamma Phi—something or other. Honestly, I couldn't remember, and I didn't care. They were all the same to me anyway.

"Who knows? Playing darts with the guys, I think," I said sardonically. Hopefully, they were using his head as the dartboard.

"You two make up?" she asked, raising her eyebrows.

"I think you misunderstood me, sweets. When I said, 'Who knows,' I meant, who cares. I hope someone throws a dart that sticks right in his egotistical ass," I corrected her, not feeling very appreciative of the guy who was supposed to be my current boyfriend. Of course, after only two dates, it didn't seem right to fall into that trap, as far as I was concerned.

She laughed, taking a long drink from her beer before answering. "Another one bites the dust," she continued, holding up her beer to toast.

"Cheers," I answered, shrugging, feeling no further comment was necessary. I twisted the cap off my beer as I surveyed the rowdy crowd around us. The decibel level at frat parties was always nothing less than near deafening. Not that I was complaining. I was in my element; the louder it got, the better. This was the kind of scene I didn't see when I still lived at home and went to community college near Woodfalls. Going to an actual university was like stepping into another world. A world that I took to immediately. I was loud and raucous, so what?

Cameo and I left the kitchen and headed outside to the patio, which gave us a front-row seat to all the action. The guys were entertaining the crowd by trying to one-up one another with one crazy stunt after the next. We'd already seen some idiot jump from the porch on the second floor, hugging a mattress. Cheers erupted on the front lawn as people hooted and hollered, yelling scores for his landing. He stood up with his arms raised in victory before bowing at the waist and tossing his cookies splendidly on two unsuspecting girls who stood off to the side. Both girls shrieked with disgust, which only invited more cheers from the onlookers.

Not to be outdone, a group of girls decided to get in on the action when the guys initiated a girl-on-girl mud-wrestling tournament. Within minutes of being soaked by hoses spilling water at full blast, the front lawn of the fraternity house was a sopping mess. Judging by the steady line of participants that had quickly formed, the nominated contestants seemed to be too drunk to care about being subjected to male gawking, or the fact that it was too cold to be rolling around like pigs in shit.

"You going?" Cameo asked.

"Hell no," I answered, choosing to keep my seat on the sidelines.

I'd been there, done that, and I didn't relish taking an elbow in the nose or having a handful of my hair pulled out to entertain drunken college guys. Chuck, who had finally appeared from wherever he'd been hiding, couldn't seem to get it through his thick head that I didn't want to participate. It took me stomping on his foot and threatening to twist his junk into a knot before he finally stopped trying to pull me into the fray.

"Aw, you mean you don't want to give your boyfriend a show and roll around and get all wet with another girl?" Cameo teased, breaking into my thoughts. She looked halfway past tipsy as she smiled at me.

We had been at the party for an hour and were nursing our third beer each. I could hold my liquor better than Cameo, who was a bit of a lightweight. Chances were I'd be dragging her ass home later since she'd barely be able to walk. She and I had made a pact when we first became roommates that we would never leave the other behind, unless of course a hot guy was involved. Little did I realize when I made the pact that it would be me shouldering most of the load.

Honestly, I didn't mind. I loved Cameo to death. I had completely lucked out when I found her as a roommate after being accepted into the University of Maine's business program. I got in by the skin of my teeth since I wasn't exactly what you would call an "academic all-star." I had taken a full year off after high school because I hadn't known what I wanted to do with my life. Finally, my mom talked me into at least trying community college, and somehow, I managed to drill into my hard-ass head that if I wanted to transfer to a state university, I would have to work hard. Not that I wasn't still having fun at the same time. I wasn't dead after all. My acceptance letter came at the perfect time. My best friend, Brittni, had moved to Seattle, and I was feeling lost without her. She was the voice of reason I didn't have that kept me in line for the most part, but without her, my antics in Woodfalls hit an epic scale. After some of the shit I'd pulled over the years, I think the entire town let out a collective sigh of relief when I moved away for school. Now, in the almost two years that I've been at UMaine, I've managed to bring my reputation as a bit of a hell-raiser with me.

I pulled my thoughts back to Cameo, who was still waiting for my answer. "Please, you know I'd have no problem throwin' down in there. It's just too damn cold to roll around in the mud," I said confidently. "Besides, Chuck's been working to get in my pants. Little does he know, the Vagmart store is closed to his ass."

"Ha, your vag-store," Cameo snorted, setting her beer on an end table that was already overflowing with bottles. "Guys are so predictable. They think all chicks wanna get naked with each other and have pillow fights."

"Well, I know that's all I think about," I said, wagging my eyebrows at her suggestively.

"Gross. You perv," she said, slapping my arm.

"Oh, come on. You know you want this," I teased, running my hands down my curvy figure. I had to sidestep a couple who were too busy sucking each other's faces as they walked to watch where they were going. "Hey, get a room," I called after them as they stumbled into the wall.

"Where the hell do you think we're going?" the guy asked, dislodging his lips long enough to answer.

"Sorry, shit, carry on then," I said, grinning at Cameo.

"See, that's why we will never have a party at our apartment," she stated.

"What, you don't want an orgy to break out on your bed?"

"Don't even finish wherever your perverted mind was headed with that," she advised, holding up her hand like a crossing guard.

I laughed loudly. Cameo was the perfect roommate in most aspects, but she did have a bit of an obsessive-compulsive personality, much to my amusement. Not that I didn't agree with her. I didn't want drunken college peeps using my bed to get nasty in either.

"Could it be you're just bummed that your bed hasn't seen any action in how many days now?" I teased, wincing as I watched two girls in the mud pit go for each other's hair. Why did girls always do that? Why couldn't we fight like men? With fists and punching instead of hair pulling and scratching. I'd much rather take a punch to the gut than have a handful of my hair pulled out.

"Whatever, you whore. It's been four days," she answered, watching the fight with interest.

"Whoa, takes one to know one," I laughed.

"Bite me, bitch. I just like guys."

"And sex," I added.

"Yes, so what, Mother Teresa?" She grinned, throwing out her beloved nickname for me.

It wasn't like I didn't enjoy sex. She knew that. Lately, I was just more selective with who I fell into bed with. Take Jock-Strap Chuck, for example. A few months ago, I might have caved and given it up to him. But I'm getting sick of the games and acting like someone I'm not to keep a guy. I used to be a total boyfriend pleaser, especially back in high school, when I dated the same creep off and on for almost seven years. I finally called it quits once and for all about a year ago. The relationship had been toxic to say the least. Years of scathing comments about how I looked or what I did, and then he would push to have sex, only to lay a major guilt trip on me when he felt remorse after we did it. Jackson suffered from a serious case of being a momma's boy. We'd no sooner do the dirty deed than he would whimper about premarital sex and how disappointed his mother would be. Even after years of putting up with his shit, actually committing to break up with Jackson was difficult. He was my first serious boyfriend. The one I gave my virginity to, or my V-card as I liked to call it. That was a big deal to me, despite my wild-child persona and the way people perceived me on the outside. It's not like you can ever get that back, even when the guy turns out to be a douche. Jackson definitely became that and more. After what he said to me when we broke up, I was scared no guy would want me again. His words cut me deeply and made me feel like I was lacking. His mom actually threw a party when we were officially over.

After leaving the Jackson mess behind me, I eventually found the confidence to try my luck with guys again, but after a string of disastrous first dates, I began to believe that maybe Jackson had been right. He was as good as I deserved. If not that, then maybe the dating gods were punishing me for all my past sins. Like the time in seventh grade I talked Braxton Fischer into switching the video we were supposed to watch in Mr. Morton's science class with a porno he had found hidden in his dad's nightstand table. Mr. Morton made the mistake of leaving the room for almost ten minutes before he came back to see two topless, big-breasted girls washing cars on the TV.

"What the hell?" a shocked Mr. Morton had yelled as he turned several different shades of red. The class erupted with laughter, and although none of my classmates ratted me out, Mr. Morton knew better and immediately sent me to the office. I could have argued. He had no proof it was me, but my reputation had already been established.

The principal, Mrs. Jameson, called my dad to pick me up, which I thought was odd considering she knew my mom. I finally understood when he showed up and she handed over the video to my dad with a scornful look on her face, like she was repulsed to even be that close to something so unholy. She thought the video was his, but my dad didn't skip a beat. He didn't flush with embarrassment or stammer at being reprimanded. Instead, he thanked her and told her he was wondering where he had left it, leaving Mrs. Jameson looking utterly scandalized.

The only lecture I got on the way home was a reminder that some parents may not want their children to see movies about those kinds of car washes. That was the best thing about Dad. He always understood the person I was, never judging or scolding me. He would simply give reminders and pointers of what a better course of action may have been. I loved both my parents fiercely for their gentle restraints.

I wish I could tell you that was the last prank I ever pulled, but my reign of stunts continued into high school. I would pick a victim and execute my prank with the precision of a surgeon. Dad always said if I would learn to harness that power toward school, I would be a straight-A student. That would have been tragic and a complete waste of fun, in my opinion.

Eventually, I mellowed when I was dating Jackson. He reminded me countless times that his mom would never approve of me if I was always causing trouble. Little did he know, I didn't want or need his creepy mom's love.

For that reason more than any other, breaking up with Jackson had been necessary. Our relationship was like a runaway train headed for a brick wall. Unfortunately, none of my relationships after that turned out any better. My friends Brittni and Ashton said I had an uncanny gift of gravitating toward the only jerk in the crowd. I always shrugged off their comments. I dated guys who suited me, which usually meant they were as loud and wild as I was.

"Wow, did she seriously just push that girl's face into her boobs?" Cameo asked, pulling me back to the present. She stepped closer to get a better look at the two mud-covered girls, who had grabbed the attention of most of the male population at the party. As the crowd cheered the girls along, I noticed everyone watching had their cell phones out to record the wrestling match, so I pulled out mine too.

"You're not going to post that, are you?" Cameo asked as I moved in closer.

"Why the hell not? This is epic on a whole new level," I answered as one of the girls shoved the other to the ground and straddled her.

"Damn, that's hot," a warm male voice said behind me.

I grinned as I turned around, recognizing the voice of my friend Derek. "Really? I can score their numbers for you if you'd like," I joked.

"Honey, I'm talking about Tall, Dark, and Shirtless over there," he answered, pointing to a well-toned guy who had removed his shirt so it wouldn't get splattered with mud.

"Right, here I thought you had suddenly decided to bat for the other team," Cameo teased Derek, looping her arm through his.

"Sweetheart, you could only wish," he said, dropping a kiss on her forehead.

"Damn straight," she giggled. "No pun intended," she added before frowning up at him. "Why do all the good ones turn out to be gay?"

"So we can have marvelous friends like you two without the mess of a romantic relationship. Just think, if I were straight, we wouldn't be friends."

"That's because we'd be lovers," I cooed, snuggling up to his free arm.

"I love you, Tressa baby, but you'd scare me in bed," Derek said, wrapping his arm around my waist.

"Oh come on, I'd go easy on you," I answered, grinding my hips against his leg.

"Don't believe her. I swear the wall looked like it was going to collapse the last time she had a guy over," Cameo teased, sticking out her tongue at me as I swiped at her with my free hand.

"Whatever, Wonder Woman," I said, reminding her of the last guy she slept with, who had a fondness for comic books. He showed up at our apartment one night with a costume from the Halloween store. Usually, I didn't mind sticking around when Cameo had a guy over, but I had to leave for that one. The truth was, it had been months since I'd even considered being with a guy.

"Hey, what about the dude with the camera? I'm surprised you didn't take him up on it," she returned, talking about the last guy who almost made it into my bed until he wanted to record us. He had to go outside to collect his camera and clothes from the yard after I threw his belongings out the window and kicked his ass out.

"Unlike you, I only do high-class porn," I threw back.

"As stimulating as this conversation is, I'd rather be dancing," Derek said, indicating the open door of the frat house where the music had been turned up.

Cameo and I agreed, following Derek toward the music we could feel pumping through our chests. Joining a crowd that seemed to be flowing as one, we let loose and lost ourselves in the music. Dancing came naturally to our trio, and it was something we enjoyed doing together. As in, just the three of us. Being in a large crowd, we would occasionally have to put up with some drunken dude trying to grind against Cameo or me, but Derek was good at stepping in. At six foot five, he was an imposing figure who could maneuver his body wherever he wanted to shelter us from unwanted advances.

After an hour, we were dripping with sweat, despite the nip in the nighttime air that circulated through the open windows and doors. Pulling my damp hair off the back of my neck, I indicated with a nod to Derek and Cameo that it was time for a break. It felt like we needed a shoehorn to squeeze through the jumbled bodies, but eventually we made it out of the room.

"Holy shit, talk about a cardio workout. I should be a twig after all that," I complained, snagging another drink. "I should effing hate you," I said, glaring at Cameo, who was practically a waif standing next to me.

"Don't be an ass. I'd take your boobs any day over these,"

she retaliated, cupping her smallish breasts in her hands. "At least you've got curves. I'm like a stick."

"Look, ladies, you can both be jealous of my perfect body," Derek interrupted, making a point of tossing his imaginary long hair. "Some of us got it, and some of us don't." Cameo and I laughed. Derek was a bit of a showboat, which made him perfect for our group. "I'm going to get a drink," he added, following behind Cameo, who was already headed in that direction.

I stayed behind, content with another beer I had pulled from a nearby cooler. It was nice to take a breather and observe the crowd a little. I became preoccupied watching a group playing a distorted version of Spin the Bottle when a pair of arms reached around my stomach, pulling me roughly against a hard chest.

"Are you ready to kiss and make up?" Chuck growled in my ear. He smelled like a distillery.

"Not really," I answered, stepping out of his grasp.

"Come on, girl. You're gonna let a little fight ruin this?" he said, sounding plastered.

I wanted to laugh, but that would probably have only egged him on further. I also wasn't in the mood for a messy scene tonight, so I went with a softer approach and a little more tact than he probably deserved.

As I spun around to face him, I couldn't for the life of me remember why I had gone out with him in the first place. He was a partier like I was and seemed cool when I met him at Club Zero a couple weeks ago, but he was a meathead. I pretty much realized on our first date that we probably weren't going to make it. Mostly because he was a perpetual nut scratcher. I don't mean he would do the occasional subtle shift that some guys do with their junk. If that was all he did, I could have lived with it. He was an all-out ball scratcher and didn't seem to care who saw him do it. It could be the waitress who looked disgusted as she handed over our pizza, or Cameo, or basically anyone who was having a conversation with him. If you stood next to Chuck, at some point you would see him scratch his balls.

"Chuck, it's not you, it's me," I said, cringing at the cliché I chose. How did you tell someone you would rather gouge out your eyes than see him play with his junk again?

"What the fuck? Who uses a bullshit line like that?" he declared, grabbing my arm so I couldn't move. I looked down at his hand, which was wrapped around my wrist. Seriously? Why did it always come down to this? Did I have the words *please manhandle me* tattooed on my forehead?

I saw Derek approaching from the corner of my eye. He wasn't hard to miss because of his size, and judging by the look on his face, Chuck wanted no part of what was coming. I held out my free hand to stop him before he could get involved. I may have an uncanny knack for dating assholes, but I also knew how to take care of myself when I needed to. I stepped on Chuck's shoe and slowly rolled my weight so my platform heels sank down on the softness of his toes. "In case you're too stupid to notice, we're done." He grunted in pain, making me smile. Sometimes it paid not to be a lightweight.

"Get off me, you bitz," he slurred. He wobbled to the point where I could have pushed him over.

"Why don't you go sleep it off?" Derek insisted, as he stepped in and pulled me protectively against him. This was why Derek was the best kind of friend. He wasn't a fan of violence, but you would never know it when it came to Cameo and me. Back home, I had always been the protector when it came to my friends. It was kind of nice to have a knight in shining armor. Not necessary, but still sweet. I found it endearing that even though he'd only known me for a year, he acted like we were lifelong friends. Derek was a perk that came with Cameo picking me to be her roommate last year. When I had transferred to UMaine, I knew I didn't want to do the whole dorm thing. Living at home my first two years of college made me yearn for more independence. I wanted to let loose without so many restrictions. Living in an apartment with Cameo had provided the freedom I was looking for, and sharing her best friend, Derek, sweetened the deal.

Chuck looked like he wanted to retaliate, but in the state he was in, he was in no shape to attempt anything more. With a shake of his head and a look of bewilderment in my direction, he staggered off, scratching his junk the entire time.

"Honey, you sure can pick 'em," Derek said, shaking his head with amazement before turning away from the train wreck.

"You're a fine one to talk," I pointed out, punching him in his bicep. If it seemed like I was being picky at the moment when it came to guys, Derek was even worse. He claimed he didn't feel like wasting time on meaningless relationships. I think he missed the memo on what college dating was supposed to be.

"I'm searching for someone who understands me," he said dramatically, making us laugh. "Speaking of which, hello, Clark Kent," he added, looking toward the front door. "He looks like he could understand everything I have to offer."

Cameo and I pivoted around to see who had managed to snag Derek's attention. He could be a bit of a snob when it came to man candy. Anyone who caught his eye had to be something worth seeing.

"Oh, hell no," I muttered under my breath. He was the last person I expected to see at a party like this.